praise for DAY:

"What can one say about a masterpiece? Refi[...]
journey in the Gospels with the contemporary queer experience—very often
the author's own—Anthony Oliveira commingles the earthly and the divine
in a deliciously daring work that defies categorization. God is love, we are
told, and *Dayspring* celebrates and interrogates that love in all its forms,
illuminating the sacred and the profane in equal measure. Bracing and
breathtaking, it is a glorious gift to the soul and the senses. This is a
magnificent debut!"   —David Demchuk, author of *Red X*

"Are you ready to be saved, slain, and resurrected by the power of the written
word? Are you ready to redefine the meaning of sacredness in the name of all
that is queer and holy? It is time to read *Dayspring* by Anthony Oliveira. This
incredible work of verse not only defies genre, but reinvents it entirely, bending
space and time to tell the story of Christ (as you have always imagined, but
never seen Him) and the disciple he loved in poetic language that evokes all
the passion of the Psalms. Astonishingly beautiful and unrepentantly sexy,
this is a book that is sure to both heal and challenge its readers in all the most
important ways. To open its pages is to open your heart to a vision of love
that is as deeply, tragically, and courageously human as it is divine."
            —Kai Cheng Thom, author of *Falling Back in Love with Being Human*

"Anthony Oliveira's literary debut delivers a deluge of erotic and sensuous
love that challenges our expectations of religious devotion. 'the body is a
leaky vessel' announces the beloved disciple in a melancholic meditation on
the crucifixion, and *Dayspring*, in all its carnality, overflows with the passion
of Oliveira's appeal for a Christian love that is unapologetically queer. In a
masterful display of literary experimentation that explodes the boundary
between verse and prose and that shuttles its readers between pre- and
postmodernity, *Dayspring* highlights the eroticism of the Christian mystical
tradition and, like Hadewijch, Mechthild, and Teresa before it, teaches that
ecstatic love can be both joyful and excruciatingly painful, sacred and
profane, human and divine."
            —Kris J. Trujillo, Assistant Professor, Department of Comparative
                    Literature and Director of Studies, Center for the Study
                        of Gender and Sexuality, The University of Chicago

"Reading *Dayspring*, I found myself reminded of how I read the Bible as a closeted queer teenager: Alternating between re-reading a passage over and over, finding resonance in one moment and dissonance in another, and feverishly skipping around, opening pages at random to see what gift or curse each had for me. Picking it up at times in search of comfort, at others in search of confrontation; sometimes with irritation, sometimes with a desperate hunger. If there's another way to read this utterly unclassifiable book, it evaded me. *Dayspring* confounds, challenges, and reveals like only a sacred text can."

—Chris Stedman, author of *IRL* and *Faitheist* and writer and host of *Unread*

"*Dayspring* is a grand experiment of language and queer love that succeeds on every level. Oliveira's prose is heartfelt and poignant, climbing to grand heights while weaving in his his quieter moments of fresh and sly dialogue. The love in this book is the sacred made flesh and genuine, relatable in a way scripture rarely touches. In short, this is a masterpiece."

—Chip Zdarsky, writer of *Batman* (DC Comics), *Daredevil* and *Spider-Man* (Marvel Comics), and co-creator of *Sex Criminals*

DAYSPRING

DAYSPRING

the disciple whom he loved
neaniskos
notes towards a revelation
the young man in white
a chapbook
a theophany
a gospel
a great blasphemy
against the heretic cerinthus
a breviary
a hymnal
a memoir
a work of plagiarism
an account of the word made flesh

anthony oliveira

STRANGE
LIGHT

Library and Archives Canada Cataloguing in Publication data
is available upon request

ISBN: 978-0-7710-0382-0
ebook ISBN: 978-0-7710-0383-7

Cover design: Jennifer Griffiths
Cover art: (left image) Saint John the Evangelist (1793) François-André Vincent (French, 1746-1816)/Artvee; (right image) Jorge Fuentes/Stocksy; (back cover) detail from Madonna and Child with Saint Catherine of Siena and a Carthusian Donor (Italian, Lombard (probably Pavia)) Robert Lehman Collection, 1975/The Metropolitan Museum of Art, New York; (flaps) Koersbriefje met de prijzen van de aandelen (1720) anonymous/Rijksmuseum
Printed in India

Published by Strange Light,
an imprint of Penguin Random House Canada Limited,
a Penguin Random House Company
www.penguinrandomhouse.ca

10 9 8 7 6 5 4 3 2

for the unnamed
and
    for the renamed

in the beginning was the word

    and the word was with god
    and the word was god

        and all things were made by him and through him
        and without him was not any thing made that was made

    and the word was life
    and the life was the light of all

    and the light is a light that shines in darkness
    and the darkness comprehended it not

and the word spiralled outward

    into a cosmos of orbits and counter-orbits
    into a hundred billion subjectivities
    into a trillion perspectival inquiries and organizing principles
        like lights through cracks
        like lancets through the skin

    and from the word came an array of matter and energy interfluxing
        a dazzling bewildering volatile orrery
        a wondrous widening gyre

        a going forth to multiply

and the word became flesh
    coarse hair
    crooked smile
    the taste of salt on his clavicle

    i am the disciple whom he loved

when i remember what came before, i see a black sky, a flash, and then a sound like the roar of rushing waters

i lay sprawled in the tangle of rope thick and bristled in the stern of my father's boat. the wood by now is dry, wherever its carcass is beached and whatever now scuttles there, but then it stank of its hundred hauls of ancient fish, its cedar hull lazily sweating gum to mat the hair on my legs

all day and into night we had caught nothing. half-dozing, i stared at a costive sky while my brother, stripped to the waist in the heat (but still wearing his silly hat, all the lanker for the atmosphere's dense press), minded the net. he whistled a song of my mother's. i remember her singing it, but not now its words. i remember her singing it, but not quite her voice

i wasn't there when my brother died. i am thankful for that. so many of us have sown our bones in fields remote—seed against a harvest none of us will live to glean

instead i remember that sticky, grey morning before everything, seeing from prone the desperate throb of light stagger in zigzag, and hearing my brother laugh as the humid summer air at last cracked open and drenched us cold and clean

"come and see!" and i saw: the whole sea's skin rippling with the rain's contusions, and beneath it a net swarming with silver life

tell me a story

     after that? aren't you tired? didn't you, i mean i thought—

    no, i did
obviously

i touch his hand to the stickiness on his stomach, now growing cool and
    tacky in his hair

     oh right. ok. um, in the beginning there was the

    not that. a real one

     . . . ok. ok. so. the night i was born there . . . there were a lot of
     animals. it doesn't matter why

    ok

     ok. so there were doves in rafters high, and sheep with curly horn,
     and uh, a cow all white and red and a donkey shaggy and brown

    around a baby? were you born in a

     very funny. so it was *cold*, because it was winter—

wait

i open my eyes and pull my head away from the fuzz of his chest

    when is your birthday?

     midspring, when the shepherds are in the field. that'll be
     important later. listen; never mind. it was cold, because it was
     christmas

he pushes my head back to his chest not altogether gently and starts to
    trace slow curlicues into the back of my hair

so i was shivering my baby ass off. so my mom asked the animals to help

what the fuck dude
    i whisper, softly, into the pleasant stink of his armpit

listen—so the cow blew his breath all soft and warm

    her breath

    what?

    cows are girls

    oh. right. ok whatever. moooooooo. cattle lowing, all that good stuff. so i blessed the cow

    sure

    but the fucking *donkey—eyy-onh, eyy-onh*. super cold whinnying. you know, like donkeys do

    do donkeys do that?

    of course they do that. haven't you met a donkey?

    i mean, i guess. i mostly fished

so i go up to the donkey—

    as a baby?

    so i go up to the donkey. and i say "what's your name?" but he just keeps going *eyy-onh, eyy-onh* all cold. so i pull his ears wayyyyy up and say "your name is DONKEY"

    and that's why donkeys have long ears. it might also be why mules are infertile; i might be confusing the details, and it might be funnier in portuguese

i roll away from his side and out along the length of his arm, to bring my face to rest inside his open hand, and stare out into the darkness beyond our little light

let me see if i have this right. so donkeys didn't have long ears until you, as a baby, punished them for breathing on you too coldly?

i mean . . .

I am the Way the Truth and the Light. the infinite utterance which
speaks all being into being and so am unbound by the laws of cause
and effect, chronology and chemistry, space and time, so . . .

why did all the donkeys have to be punished for that one donkey

who was only doing what you made him to do?

dude
that is kind of my whole deal

is that a true story?

of course it is. I am the Way the Truth and the—

did that really happen

oh. no

this bedtime story sucks

tell me a better one

i am kneeling on the shore tying knots in the nets by my father's skiff when i hear the scuff of you behind me huddle-housed in your sweatshirt stained with crying and dirt. long in the wilderness lost to lenten entertainments. between the patched and scudding cirrus the sun's light pours like radioactive grout

      you came back

i had to think

i think it's time to go. start. leave

and from the depths of a linty pocket you offer a hand to me that in the years short years to come i would kiss until i knew its every callus and curve. until the romans broke it, as they break everything, and left it a mangled pulp for us to scrape from their torture post. until the angels made it incorruptible and beneficent sign for all to see. until both left it perfect and golden and alien and unrecognizable to me

      will you come with me?

i look up past your arm outstretched as behind you, brow creased in beseeching, rosy-fingered dawn is unstitching night's design and the short dark bramble of your hair catches what the sky could not, the fugitive light antler-tangled there along with the grit and camp smoke and you left me and i ache like an uncracked knuckle to hike down your ratty sweatpants and kiss the constellation of moles crushed under your waistband above your thick black bush and take the whole of you unwashed from the wastes into my mouth and i knew and know that i am lost to this to you forever

and you pull me up from my knees into your chest and a whooshing head-rush echo comes into my ears that does not die away but swells into the sound itself and i say or perhaps do not say

              break my heart
              as many times as you need to

              i am yours

here at last is the thing that i was made for

      come on. get your brother. we have work down the road

      what could i do
         but follow straight?

in the dark
unseen
until it is too late to stop

    that is how seeds grow

we are dancing at a wedding
your mom had asked in that gentle tiptoe way of hers if you thought i might
like to come and then she left a space wide as an ocean for you to tearfully
relate to her in tv special tones what she had always known about what you
and i did at our furtive sleepovers tangled like stupid puppies rubbing the
snouts of our crotches together while the blockbuster video haul amused
itself onscreen
but you just said yeah! and bolted for the phone
and i rummaged for a suit that fit and the best excuse i could find and
suddenly we were
dancing through the fog machine, avoiding where a toddler dropped their
cake in a long abjected smear, and you giggled at my shy stiffness and used
your big hands to guide my hips as you pushed your lips into a raspberry
dyed red from our half-stolen wine leaving between us ever-shrinking
room for the holy spirit

and suddenly your mom is at your elbow

they're out of booze

and a cloud goes over your face and i feel suddenly i am playing with a
thunderstorm, playing with a kitten. dandled in your beautiful velveted paws

>that is not my problem
>let me have a little longer

so she touches the polyester of my shoulder with a kind squeeze, her
perfume discounted and clean and lingering
and her heels which she was nervous about but are very cute click away
and with the tempest still on your brow you lean in to whisper hot
sweet breath into the porches of my ear

>ah fuck it let's do a miracle

and you tell the wait staff to ladle out the brown dishwater from the dingy
trough of their shiny industrial hotel sink

>ok but definitely don't tell them where you got this
>and if you could not mention me in particular
>that would also be super

later, as the partygoers get drunk on the lord's vintage, fresh and unmixed
    through the kitchen door, under the stairwell's fluorescent lights
    you mutter to me sweetly
    wiping every tear from my eye
    and the eager drool from my chin

    as on my knees, clutching the firm flesh of pimpled buttocks

      i try not to scrape god's perfect cock with my teeth

one time he got really fucking furious at a fig tree

just absolutely screamed at it for
like forty-five minutes

from silence speaks the light. in the beginning was the word

the symptom of language then is reality

we speak these stories these stories speak us over and over until i am not sure if we are anything but history indulging a bad habit

we are the atoms of history dust that has gathered on sandals. and dust upon sandals, and dust upon the road

     all dies
     and all dries
     and who knows the revolutions of dust?

     my mind is not what it was
         let me try again

incarnation means nothing more than in the meat
and it was the meat of him i loved
    red and raw
    the stinking sweating heft

a father commanded his two sons to work
in the vineyard

    yes father, said one, but did not go
    no father, said the other, but he went

        which of these, then
        has done his father's will?

i thought when you asked that i knew. but i was
young then

now i am old
old as you never were nor ever will be

and i know now that love sometimes makes a
promise it cannot keep

        and sometimes no toil can fix the
        clockwork of a heart dropped from the
        mantel skittering glass across the floor

        sometimes you must say *yes* when you
        mean *no*
        there is a kindness
        that you never learned in the lie

ok a story

once upon a time a nun on an important mission was
crossing a river with her donkey laden with supplies

and the beast stumbled, and it sent all her goods,
her clothes, her books, tumbling into the stream

and as she tried to recover her ruined things i
appeared on a rock
and i said:

> that, teresa
> (because her name was teresa)
>> is how i treat all my friends
>
> and that, lord
> (she said, robes soaked in the water)
>> is why you have so few of them!

**hmm. that story *also* is not very nice
and it's kind of the same story as the donkey one**

yes

> they all are. the same story

I saw an angel nearby, in bodily form, on my left. He was marvellously
beautiful—not particularly tall, but quite short, and his
face shone as though he were of the highest of the
angels, those who seem to be all ablaze

in his hands he held a long golden spear, and at the iron tip of its shaft
I saw a gout of flame

and suddenly he thrust this, over and over, through my heart, penetrating
me to my bowels. And when he drew out the spear he
seemed to draw them with it, leaving me on fire, with
a wondrous love for god

the pain was excruciating, and I moaned and cried out

and yet it was so surpassing sweet that still I want
nothing else

for how can the soul be content with less than god?

—saint teresa of avila
translated from the spanish

he sits in a house cool and dark as the mob presses in. from my post amid the knit of the crowd outside I hear the scratch of his barked laugh tumbling over their bodies like a brook breaking over thirsty stone. a twinge of jealousy dances over my ribs for a second, and is gone

a street away there is a bustle. men, square and strong, with a beauty that is familiar and a cruelty that is not, are moving through the press, entitled and rough. with them is a woman—his mother, older now but not yet old, who watches the crowd part like she is afraid, but not for herself, and not quite of them. as the young men jostle on her behalf, from her scarf falls a serpent-coil of hair: the same unmistakable tawny brown as his, the same precise, nervous choreography of her sudden gesture to tuck it back behind her ear

she looks at me as she waits outside, and I smile with an apologetic wince and remember her thousand kindnesses to me at kitchen tables and graduations and when I turned up tear-stained with a backpack on her front porch asking if I could stay the night and she swooped me in and carefully asked nothing at all and fetched clean ninja turtle sheets. her perfume like faded roses. the eldest of her worried entourage barks into the house, barks with a bark so much like his, slightly shrill to mask his nerves. james was my brother's name too

in reply from inside the house, I hear the burble of his voice, its words indistinct, and a laugh cascade lazily again through the crowd. he will not see her

in front of me her eyes are still staring, glassing now, and I feel the heat in my cheeks, the embarrassment he never seems to have the decency to feel, that has left me a raw nerve and forever seeping apologies in his wake. but today, for her, i have none

and i know: this is how he will leave me too. a swift, cruel blow that will shatter all my bulk. a surgical strike from above, hurling masonry through the streets like leaves of concrete. i will scream, desperate in the temple precincts, looking for a lost boy i had mistook for kind, who will laugh at my panic: didn't i know he should be with his father?

and the learned and the holy will praise his wit, and his insight, and the bravery with which he left us behind. he will skewer steel through the raw pulsing meat of my heart, to wild acclaim

i watch his brothers swear and push their way back out of the crowd, the sweat darkening their shirts. she glances once, hopefully, over their broad, desultory backs shaped so much like his, and i realize i recognize their cruelty after all

what you ask for you will get
what you look for you will find

and if the door is not yet open
pound harder

the dimensions of hell are empty and
            all her perverted pageantries are here!

rowing arms and full broad backs seized with lactic the
storm swooping down from the hills like a grinning
coyote a roaring raging surge bodychecking the boat
bent on capsize shaking leathered fig-fruit from the
bough to send us all sprawling stark into the spray into
pliant mud and glutted catfish beneath a soundless sea

and then i see you stride across the moonlight

the waves playing rugby all around you

            rain hissing and spitting against a
phosphorus corona

a god of sodium light

wake up

please wake up

the grass is cool and damp from the night air and the broad flat
carpenter pads of his hand are smoothing my hair too roughly. i fell
asleep

when did i fall asleep?

his nose against my face is slick. a dog, pawing, whimpering. even in
the dark i can see his eyes are wild and wet and his brow soaked and
chilled. through the slit of my white sindon my baffled, dozy erection
nudges, which he is cupping desperately and absently. i sleepily try to
pull him down to me before i process something is wrong

listen

nearby peter's snores rumble the stone while my brother sleeps face up,
open-mouthed, gulping lazily like a dying trawl. then above their bass i hear
it: a troop of men, clanking and cursing, are coming up the garden path

what if we ran

yes we could run. we would lose peter i would lose my brother but i have lost
everything for him before lost mother and father and town the children and
wife and dignity i will never have and i cannot care to miss—just dust on the
road behind us

what would it profit a man to lose his soul just to save some petty world

but suddenly there is light everywhere as torches catch the vicious crags of
faces. there is a boot in my gut and i am hauled from the turf

"which of these faggots is it?" they throw the snivelling little crabapple traitor
into the ash around our cold fire and he scrambles and sobs and clutches at
his master's cheek seeping mewled apologies and frantic slobber kisses

with a rage i did not know i had i tackle the miserable grimy spy and the guards' arms are everywhere on me but the linen is loose their armour is heavy and on him they have not yet even laid a finger and suddenly peter is awake and roaring, brandishing a sword i did not know he had the sense to carry

"we run," i whisper to him while peter holds their attention, sliding from my sleeves, his forehead to mine. "if they kill us they kill us but we run now"

in his eyes i see the light that lit the stars the dark that sat brooding upon the waters and

i have loved you more than i have loved anything. you can't forget

Never. Never. the whole of my life before and since i have broken every promise i ever made so that i might more perfectly serve that one

and so i bolt, wriggling from the white robe in the soldier's hands, slipping from the net like a flash of living mercury. naked and shining and laughing, to be so free

(at least saint ambrose believed it was me)

but when i turn breathless on the hilltop, he is not with me. instead there he stands rooted, right where i left him, stalwart and righteous as a Goya by their torchlight. still not a hand upon him

not a man had followed. no one had cared
and i crumble naked in the grass
and weep

and when the torches clink their way i follow
crawling like a garden snake through the moonlit world

i return to the spot in the morning after haunting the margins of the show trials and interrogations and indignities and the sun is hot. nearby from a tree hangs the traitor, the cord of his belt around his neck, his expression an ugly scarlet bloat. upon his brow is a wound i might well have given him. soon his blotching face will split like sweet rotting fruit and the birds of the tree are inquisitive but not yet brave enough to feast

i take his piss-stained clothes and stumble into town to watch the world end

still i keep my testament

there was a word
    i echo

i am supposed to write. supposed to claw into the rock of history some
phrase that will last when i am dead and gone and though all the world
cannot conjure the contours of my face it will remember the flinty brilliance
that i sparked here in the dark alone and the rock of his majesty against
which i struck that light

but my heart is so broken
broken is not even right. it is a pulverized thing. a bruised, uncabled tissue,
its fibres relaxed and purpling with pooling cooling curdling blood. fruit
rotting to succulence

when i sleep i remember days that never were. i dream a life i never saw and
which i now see he never wanted

did you not know i would be in my father's house?

       he left, and i do not know what now becomes of me

we are supposed to endure. but the truth of history the real fact of the
       record is shuffling uncertainly off a dimming stage
       recorded only in the footnote
       half-remembering half-remembered
       plausibly deniable or plainly denied

       it can't mean that so it doesn't mean that
       and it's all forgotten
       while the snow of history falls on the living and the dead

writing does not heal. the document does not make whole. poesis is not a
therapy it is thrusting a filthy digit into the spot where the lance has
pierced you and it says:

       look, here. ascend and transcend all you like; this is the wound that
       will not close

touch the plunging suppuration
and learn when love is like an abscess left to rot

       this is the precise spot
              you have been marred forever

how is it that they could kill him but
i am what died

i watch them drive a rivet through a foot that i kissed
i know not how oft

feet i cooled and washed with my own hair: the
delicate, beautiful ball of his ankle, swooping to
curve down into ridges dusted with errant tufts of
hair, a faint sourness from leather and dirt and the
thoughtless joy with which he walked and ran and
even once danced, scooping me up in his arms in a
nighttime waltz in an upper room when all the
world was asleep and there was no music but my
jackhammering chest and i asked him in a child's
whisper to draw shut a window curtain lest the
neighbours see and which to my secret thrill he did not

smashed and ruined and unmade

be as kind to others as you are to yourself
be as kind to yourself as you are to others

that's it

so why do you hate donkeys so much

i don't hate donkeys

> he is dandling my fingers in the space above our heads, as dust
> plays in the light

i love donkeys
donkeys are cute, and they do their best, and they end up hobbled, maimed,
broken in a stream

> they try
> and they fail

every day a stress test
> till breakdown

to be a donkey is to know the truth:

> God always gives us more than we can handle

> he presses his finger into the centre of my hand

ok. well, i like the nun

i thought you would

> good night

> and he kisses me on the forehead
> and in his arms i dream of the smell of hay
> and the breath of beasts

there is no greater love than this:

  to lay down your life
  for your friend

But when a deep consideration had from the secret bottom of my soul drawn
together and heaped up all my misery in the sight of my heart, there arose a
mighty storm, bringing a mighty shower of tears

in the new wing of the school, still under construction, where the repeating
blue and ugly yellow bricks of the building grew more haphazard, there was
a makeshift alcove where a window used to be, now boarded up into a sort
of wooden recessed bench. i would sit there hiding, as i always hid, reading
in this nook at lunch after third-period science

the plywood smelled of pine and chemicals and then: there you were

in the flesh

    hi! what are you reading?

you scrambled in beside me without asking my name or if you could as my
brain sounded alarms and now the plywood mingled with cheap teenage
cologne and under it the ruddy cheerful b.o. of your uniform blazer whose
infrequent dry cleanings could not compete with football practice and the
poutine you had at lunch and the orange your locker mate had lost
somewhere in the back of november

    so many clones!

you had taken the vivid comic book from me. on the cover a figure his
head wool-white his eyes flame and his feet like brass and he thumbed
through it

    i guess he's back, but it's not the same
    you can't just keep bringing them back it's cheating

    yeah. it's pretty awful
    the art too. and you smiled like we had a secret and i felt my whole
face flush like it would pour with blood

can i read with you. but it's so bad. so?

    who cares
    it's still good

for the time is at hand

        behold, he cometh with the clouds: first begotten of the dead
                and every eye shall see
                and every ear shall hear
            and those who pierced him shall wail

i am alpha and omega, begun and end
which is, and which was, and which is to come

            his hair was white as wool, as white as snow
            and his eyes were as a flame of fire
            and his feet like unto fine brass, as if they burned in a furnace
            and his voice as the sound of many waters

and in his right hand seven stars
and out of his mouth a sword
and his countenance was as the sun shineth in his strength

once there was a man who found a pearl
    and sold everything he had for it

    because it was priceless

i get off the subway three stops from school on a saturday and walk, checking addresses, till i find the small house that must be yours and you open the door wide before i am even up the stairs to knock wearing just your underwear and a t-shirt that stops too short and you say

oh hey! come in

you bring me to the kitchen table where your mom says hi and goes upstairs to fold laundry and i ask indiscreetly about your dad and you just say gone and siblings sometimes and your math textbooks are all disgorged like error disembowelled barfing quadratics to carpet her cave and a gigantic green parrot is in a cage the size of a small apartment in the corner of the room

oh! does he talk?

you look at him, frowning, as though this is a perplexing thought that has never occurred to you, and you say

no, he is a bird

and the parrot looks at me accusingly as though i have nearly betrayed some terrible confidence, silently warning me not to expose a strange grift whose contours i have not quite conceived

and we sit for ninety minutes, as i try very hard not to look at your lap at the dented curve of your y-front basket red piping against white like a beautiful scuffed baseball tucked between your legs smashed against the chipped-paint pine of the seafoam kitchen chair only eighteen inches below us, and we stare at the math you do not understand as i point with a mechanical pencil that is the colours of a normal pencil in some strange baudrillardian echo of the real staring at geometries still not staring at the imprint of your dick and the parrot gingerly grooms itself and sits in solemn silence as though it too might be failing math and is determined to turn the semester around and you fart loudly twice against the chair like the crackle of cheap plastic of supermarket baked goods jostled and beep sorry! without the slightest shame

and you say

i think i get it

so this part hath lines and a middle mark which thou seest common
to both going apart coming together raised up on high dancing [vox
nihili] of three signs like in kind [vox nihili] balanced equal in measure

and i say, um not really, and you say

oh whatever i'm bored let's watch tv

and you tumble an avalanche down the basement stairs and crash over the
lip of the couch and you turn on football and i admit mortified i don't
understand it and you explode happily like a pinata now i can teach you!
and suddenly

your head is in my lap

babbling about end zones, pointing excitedly at various men in various
configurations, the perfect seashell of your ear full of the endless immensity
of the sea (and a few flecks of amber wax) in front of me as i grow terrified
you can feel me hardening a half inch from your gentle head rising like an
elbow to menace the socket of your eye, and for some reason you are telling
me about who on our high school football team jacks off the most (it is marc
g., who says he did it seven times once when his parents were out of town),
and suddenly your hand is on my bicep for some reason just sort of half
gripping and you are looking up at me from my lap from under perfect
eyelashes and your mom brings down cookies which you scarf three at a time

and then it is time to go home

and i say bye to the bird who does not say it back but i can tell at least thinks
about it and you chirp bye! from your porch still in your underwear and i
trudge back to the subway

the thick world in its rotundity struck flat
my thick tongue at the altar struck dumb

half-tumesced and baffled and obliterated

the canticle of the sun
        among the notes of saint francis of assisi

altissimus, omnipotent, good great Lord

        and yours alone

        none is worthy to speak the name unspoken
        the name we break and share among us

so praise the Sun our brother
        day-bringer, light-giver
        beautiful and radiant and splendid

so praise the Moon our sister
        luminous in her sea of stars

so praise our brother Wind
        the air, the cloud serene
        breath of the world

so praise our sister Water
        useful, humble, crystalline

so praise our brother Fire
        a comfort in darkness
        playful, handsome, and strong

so praise our sister, our mother Earth
        who feeds us, teaches us
        and who laughs in flowers

so praise our fellow children
        who forgive us, suffer with us
        and endure to see the coming crown

so praise Death
        inescapable
        and whose sting, through you, we need not fear

and so praise and bless our Lord
        whom to praise then blesses us

        amen

a child sat playing on the ford of a brook. carefully with a branch he directed the waters into channels, and gathered the waters that flowed there into pools, and with the mud that formed he sculpted twelve little clay partridges

and his father saw it, and came to him and said:

> you must not do these things, for it is the day of rest, and so it is not lawful for you to labour, neither to make anything with the work of your hands

but the little boy regarded his father and said:

> of the days of this earth
> its calendars and timetables
>   i am Lord

and he clapped his hands

> and chirping the birds took their flight

pile up the holy books like driftwood on the beach swarming with lice and
crawl with them dig and bite and try to find something to eat in the ink
and hair and you will go hungry

language picked clean to the bone

who could write love when the sediment of history is crushing to powder
to new stone
turning marvels and monstrosities to marble
instead let the mountain and the rock hide me
let the water cold and new trickle amid the dust where i finally sleep
and let the mulch of me the amber sap extruded into souvenir bottles feed
something better

love is what ruins. love is what costs. love is a flaming sword at our backs a
garden left to ruin and to wild
gone to seed

    but
    there is ruth and there is naomi
    whose vow they repeat in cheap tinsel
    not knowing the women they echo when
    they knit themselves to one another:

            where you go i will go
            and where you stay i will stay
            your people will be my people
            and your God my God

    a kingling unkinged by slingshot sling
    and ahead of me on the road: a boy a dog and an angel

            i am my beloved's, and my beloved is mine
            teeth white as sheep

                love is as strong as death
                passion fierce as the grave

                its flashes are the flashes of fire
                love is a raging flame

many waters cannot quench it
neither can all the floods come to drown it

i am lost
but even in the wilderness, i would know you

and the clouds of the sky parted, and from them descended a spirit, like unto
a dove

> that first sat brooding on the vast abyss
> and made it pregnant

> that lit the desert in its fire
> and glinted in flashes upon the swords of mighty busiris
> when the sojourners of goshen passed through the flood

> that susurrated through the velvet of a virgin's ear

> that fell like tongues of fire
> to unmake the huddled babble

> that now moved like a wind in the reeds
> to find a shivering boy dunked in the freshets of the jordan

and a voice spoke: *this is My Son, in whom I am well pleased*

> and Satan heard it

and the crowd was awed to fear, but the young man was puzzled

and he wandered into the wilderness, that he might discover what this meant

and Satan set forth slithering through the dust of this world
> to find the youth in the waste
> and to sink his venom in the tenderness of his heel

and time itself entered time
and chose for itself a birthday

the maker of adam became a man
the sun's creator felt its warmth
the ruler of the stars cried out for mother's milk
and the word itself was speechless

bread itself hungered
fountain thirsted
light winked and slept

the way grew weary from the journey
the truth accused of lies
the judge brought to trial
and justice condemned unjustly

discipline scourged with whips
foundation itself dangled from on high
courage weakened
healer wounded

and life itself did die

    —augustine of hippo

the young man sat in the barren place beneath a sky too big and wondered what it might mean to be a Son of God

since his youth he had known his difference like a tooth out of place, his tongue testing its porcelain like an oyster's pearl, a hard bright kernel readying itself to rip from flesh

he had sat among the other boys, shouting and hooting their games and tortures, and known he did not fit

known he was a piece bigger than the puzzle

known it lanceted his mother's heart, and not known why

and peering from behind the eyes of a feeding cormorant, Satan regarded the youth, and wondered what it might mean to be a Son of God

many Sons of God there had been: a beautiful riotous orgy of his brothers in gorgeous feathered copulation before the Throne

many Sons of God there had been: and a third of their host he had dragged with him down to matter's reek and Hell's chastity

what would be one more

and he approached the youth

[in the guise of a foul old man
in the guise of a beautiful swain
in the guise of a leering shaggy satyr]

and the devil said: *you are hungry—if you are the Son of God, why do you not take what you ache for?*

is the flesh of the world ripe, but not for eating? will you wait for it to slacken, let its juice drop for flies, when you might tear and be sated?

what kind of Lord would let his sons go hungry? what kind of God deny his creations what they crave?

put your mouth to the hardness of the rock, and find it soften to nourishment

but the youth said, i will not live on bread alone

once in the dark, with the DVD
menu looping, you whispered
my name and held me close and
kissed a zigzag constellation
down the meridian of my face—
five marks whose scorch i can
still feel to this day, like cinders
cast from a splitting log. like the
coal the angel pressed to Isaiah's
mouth

and you became my faith

hide a little leaven in the dough
and see how large the loaves will rise

and jonathan fell upon geba and israel became obnoxious to the philistines
but the numbers of the israelites were small and they quaked in fear
    and some fled across the jordan and were lost to gad and gilead
    while saul made sterile obsequies to the lord
        words flying up in smoke
        thoughts clung below

but his son jonathan was mighty and brave
    and at the pass of mikmash with the boy who was his armour bearer
he crept with the scent of loam in his nostrils and fell alone upon their camps
    his leather belt grappled upon slim hips
    his thick blunt sword plunged through their necks
    his wooden bow flashing in his hand
    his gleaming plate slick with philistine blood

    and the earth shook at jonathan bearing the lord heavy upon his back
    and the panic of the fear of isaac wound like clover through the
    tents of gath
    and the slaughter and the plunder were a smoke most pleasing to
    the lord

and saul in his superstitions swore oaths to prohibit that his soldiers eat
while they raided
to keep keen their hunger for the slaughter

    but in the woods jonathan found a honeycomb
    and he reached out his staff and dipped it
    and put the honey in his mouth
    and he said:

how much greater might our works have been
if not for my father's starveling madness

how sweet is the taste of honey
how brightened by its sweetness are my eyes

how much sweeter is the taste of david
forage forbid, wild-grown
whose kisses are the kisses of your mouth
who exceeds into the gutters of your lips

and the devil set the youth on the top of the highest mountain crag and showed him all the kingdoms of this world

from the ziggurats of babylon to london's tower bridge, from the ruined temple mount to the plundered oil fields of iraq

and he said: *behold: thrones, dominations, princedoms, and virtues— this world is in their power, and the powerless will never save it*

they will sweep from rome from parthia from america
locusts in crowns of gold
teeth of lions and tails of scorpions

cut your plastics
save imprudent turtles
rescue oily ducks
still they will choke your sky and poison your waters

and behold for all your labour: even the ocean itself will burn

every breath you steal from another's lungs, every bite you take from another's plate there is no escaping the bargain

what kind of God would let a world come to this?

sell yourself to me, who am its lord

do a little evil to do a greater good

there is no ethical consumption under corporeality

master the world. then you might save it

but the youth said, get behind me, satan! and there may you always walk

to live is to cast a shadow
chasing light

and the crown i need
you cannot provide

on the news i watch the cathedral of notre-dame burn
its spire falling through its roof
leaving a jagged, flaming ring yawning smoke into the parisian sky

they say among its reliquaries was your crown of thorns
one of many claimants
maybe they are all legitimate maybe you kept swapping hats all day at your
execution
costume changing like an awards show host
each successive torture device going into a box like a presidential pen

i lit a candle there once beneath its rose window
fire is part of the natural life cycle of a cathedral an architect on tv says
just history mulching itself
i still cry a little like a loser

before three days have passed the gofundmes and kickstarters have
already financed the renovation from iffy sources touting french identity
in that peculiarly french way that makes you wonder if the next sentence
will be something breathlessly racist
and i remember once i waited in line two hours to see the hand of
saint francis xavier and watched people fall down weeping at the wizened,
gnarled zombie paw under glass and gold
"the hand that baptized asia"
an ugly little miracle
the undead grasp of colonialism rotting in a little golden box

and i remember you saying:

if you are making an offering
and remember a friend you have offended
leave your gift forgotten on the altar
and go and make amends

and i imagine how much more magnificent:

     to leave the ashen ring vomiting its smoke to heaven
     let the rain and the pigeons tour the riot scene
     gravely assessing the devastation

     how much more true a relic of your crown
     to leave the bristling spiky hole in the roof
     letting heaven fall till justice was done

     what a stupid thought

and the devil saw that the youth would take neither the golden
pleasures of the world nor the iron sceptres of its kingdoms

and he beheld the young man, trembling, hungry, and alone, and
knew what at last to offer him

and he set the youth at the highest pinnacle of the temple, and he said:

> *if you are the Son of God*
> *if this world has a purpose, and you a place in it*

> *jump*

> *let it show you*

and if it means anything at all to live, you will be saved
> *the angels and archangels and the choirs of heaven will swoop like*
bats from their perches to break your fall
> *surely someone will stop you. surely some friend call just in time*

> *you will wake in the cooling bath, or your face in the sick, or in the*
bleached snugness of the hospital, clean and bright and hungry, and know
you were spared for a greater purpose:

> *a life worth living.*

> > *and if not. well.*
> > *what will it matter anyway?*

and the young man stood with his foot at the edge of the precipice

> you show me life without meaning and think it will overwhelm me
> > and it might

> but first i will show it what it could mean. then let it do what it will

> > let them see
> > on each brow a secret crown
> > on yours. on mine

> > and even if there is no God
> > let the world rise to be his children

and the devil left him
to await a more opportune time

on the desolate and pitiless plain, David stripped himself of his armour
and naked spat his curse upon the Philistine:

> *and i will give the carcasses of your host unto the fowls and beasts*
> *that all the earth may know that there is a God in Israel*

and from his sling into Goliath's skull the young shepherd drove a stone
and from atop the fallen bulk he crowed
and with the giant's own sword from his shoulders struck the beast's head

and he was so beautiful even the birds ached to behold him

and he presented the split skull and the story of his victory to Saul
the king that God had made for Israel
and to the prince his son, who was called Jonathan

and Jonathan saw him

and Jonathan's soul was knit with the soul of David
and Jonathan loved him as his own soul

I have my doubts about all this real value
in mountaineering, in getting
to the top of everywhere and
overlooking everything. Satan
was the most celebrated of
Alpine guides, when he took
the Son to the top of an
exceeding high mountain and
showed him all the kingdoms
of the earth.

But the joy of Satan in standing on a peak
is not a joy in largeness, but a
joy in beholding smallness, in
the fact that all men look like
insects at his feet. It is from the
valley that things look large; it
is from the level that things
look high; I am a child of the
level and have no need of that
celebrated Alpine guide.

I will lift up my eyes to the hills, from
whence cometh my help; but I
will not lift up my carcass to
the hills, unless it is absolutely
necessary. Everything is in an
attitude of mind; and at this
moment I am in a comfortable
attitude.

I will sit still and let the marvels and the
adventures settle on me like
flies. There are plenty of them, I
assure you. The world will never
starve for want of wonders; but
only for want of wonder.

—G.K. Chesterton, *Tremendous Trifles*, 1909

                    i will tell you the secret of secrets

at the end—the real end

when this world's dissolution shall be ripe
and purged into a conflagrant mass

                                        then will come a dawn to hell
                                             a sunlight peeping
                        through the windows of its empty broken skyscrapers
                                its dolorous mansions hollow and unhaunted
                        its doors and casements left to rattle in the blowing wind

and its first inhabitants—the gorgons, the hydras, the chimeras dire—
will peer from last dark corners to see:

that all the angels that clattered down so late with their broken
chicken wings in nine days fall

            and all the dusty souls they had for a thousand centuries
            stacked like dried cod

            will be gone

            homeward returning

and at the bottom of the beehive crater city at the heart of the
thawing lake of ancient silent ice the poor bloat dragon of
the crater of the pit of gehenna of the muddy dingy ditch

will melt
like a slug under salt, filth and leprous sin sloughing off from the
drowsy seraph underneath in warm wet sheets

for holy is the angel in moloch
and there shall be nothing lost

and then: a bright, white apricity, like spring caught in the hanging
laundry
            will light an age of endless date

and all shall be well
and all shall be well
            and every manner of thing shall be well

you were the most beautiful thing i'd
ever seen and your face was too close to
mine, acne amid short stubble and thick
eyelashes slow-blinking like the world
could wait for you to decide to come
back to it. you just never went away even
though i tried to shake you like a burr
in the pelt of a dog

turning your desk around in math class
noisily to ask me for help, talking at full
volume and mortifying me as the
teacher lectured, rocking me as i cried
by the water, screaming at me in the
rain, at comic-cons and fringe plays and
holding our urgent cocks together as we
came in quick firm tugs, mingling god's
seed with mine in thick joyful gouts as
you laughed like water

converting me unto thyself, so that i
sought neither wife, nor any hope in this
world

when jonathan saw david the world
broke open

history warped in its gravity

through the renovations of the
collapsing, decadent reign of the
paranoiac saul
a bird beating its wings in rafter high

rain to a parched landscape
relief to a flat horizon

i saw the dunker once
rinsing sins by the river
they said he was your cousin once
but it was my eyes not yours i saw
   you brought me to the edge of the jordan
   beachhead of joshua ford of elijah
   to the coolness of the riverbank
    and the whispering of the reeds
    and the light steadily strong

 and across the glass of the water of the misty mid-region of weir
 where men walked like trees i saw him:
   a bathing satyr

   the piper at the gates of dawn
and he sang:

   about willows and the lyre and the torment of the captive
    and a land made foreign by the conqueror's clutch

and you pumped my hand in the valve of yours and winked
 and kissed the sweat of my brow and said
 watch this

and you pulled your shirt over you and it hitched at your back and my fist
at instinct tangled itself in the coarse dark carpet of your belly around the
thickening base of you as your fly unzipped

 and i watched you ford the water naked to where the dunker stood

  where he drowned you

the sky cracked apart

 and god ran out like an egg

   and the golden molten yolk of him poured over you
   liquid limpid light sudden and magnificent
 like a hive breaking the stores of its nectar to anoint forth a queen

 and i your drone

 helpless trembling waiting for you to use the end of me
and i stood upon the lawn and listened to the silence of a dispersing epiphany
 the wind playing in the reeds and the rushes and the osiers

the friar came to the abbot and said:

> Father, i keep my little rule. i keep my little
> fast. my prayers i chant; my silence i observe;
> and my heart i wipe clean. what else then
> should i do?

and the abbot rose, and stretched out his
hands to heaven, and his fingers became
like ten lamps of fire

and he said:

> why not burn?

come with me, fishermen
   and i will make you fish for men

my brother James and i followed you into town
      and with us Simon, whose boat every night jostled gently against ours
in the dock and with whom we worked in jocular companionship every day
upon the hot sea glass
      and his brother Andrew, who had been a busy acolyte of the baptizer
before he fell to Herod and sent his followers scattering for old hovels and
new messiahs

i was drunk on you. intoxicated and dizzy and astonished that they should
be feeling it too. i had grown so used to the rise of this hot flush alone, as
a shame and secret—a deed done in the dark, now brought to searing light

as we walked to Capernaum they peppered you with
questions like excited jackdaws. my hand brushed
yours and you seized it—*too sweaty, too dirty, too soft,*
my brain screamed in humid alarm—and instead of
recoiling at being so public you squeezed it with a
firm, gentle pulse, and smiled at me

and as we went down the road, you went on holding it as though my
brother, these men, and the world could not see—as though you did
not care, as though they would not care, as though i would not care

and i felt the world rewire with possibility

      i was utterly lost. i was
      utterly yours

a sower goes out to sow

and some seeds fall upon the beaten path
where the birds swoop down upon them
and devour their number

and some seeds fall on stony ground
where their tender shoots sprout quickly
and rootless scorch in sun

and some seeds fall among the bramble
where they wander lost amid the thorns
and choke without the light

but some seeds fall on good ground
in a clean, well-lighted place
in a room of one's own

and all the world is filled with their branches
and their seeds are with us still

simon was rough and dumb and brawny and
beautiful. in my earliest days on the boats,
when our father first taught us, i had furtively
watched the tuft on his chest and cables of his
big broad back work beneath his damp shirt,
peeking stealthily at the thick barbs of hair
that flashed at his belly when he stretched. he
kindly pretended not to notice, or even shot a
wink when he caught me, and was quickly like
another brother to me—indeed, often
defending me guilelessly against the
fulminations of james's blacker moods

> you sensed simon's sweet lunkheadedness instantly and with a
> smile in your squint said
> i'm calling you rocky

> which andrew took to like a dog rolling in a puddle

when i see the great edifice of porphyry and gold erected rise like
a spiky hermit crab shell, unfitliest monument, in my mind's eye
i remember the supreme pontiff whom you called your stone:
one eye closed, tongue out, trying to fix a child's toy to forestall
another round of loud sobs

palinode of peter

no
i did not deny you
when the portress at the gates of night inquired
and asked if i was a galilean too
which she knew from my accent was so

      for i love you
      and i will keep your sheep

no
i did not deny you
at the charcoal fire
when sparking faces in the dark
flashed and lit my own
and recognized from braver light
the way i had laughed
as you overturned a cart
of souvenirs onto a stumbling city guard

      for i love you
      and i will feed your lambs

no
i did not deny you
when the cousin of malchus insisted
malchus whose ear i had cut like lunch meat
torn loose like a cold sow's head under butcher blade
and tossed on tile to please my cat
malchus who was a slave
who was only following orders
who i would gladly strike and tear again

      for i love you
      and i will tend your flock

for the keys are mine
to bind and loose
and the net though full
will never burst
     i am clean
     i am made new

and what you forget
let all the world forgive

and there was a man there in the church with a withered hand. and you told the man—a trembling, embarrassed boy, hair just starting to thin, eyes with the dart of a desert lizard under hawks: stand forth

and you asked of the congregation
but staring only at the boy: we are called to rest. may we not even break that rest to heal?

silence breathed
it is the day of respite—commanded by god
not an emergency
it sets a precedent you cannot maintain
many suffer worse and will go untreated
if we never pause, never reflect
we will exhaust and strain and buckle and break
there is only so much resource
only so much time

and you knew it was so
and you heard their august silence, pregnant in portent and the sad justness of its sentence
old men in their wisdom
always know precisely
how much the young should suffer

and you met the boy's darting, pleading eyes, silent as a wound
and said:

it is not reasonable
let us, then, be the end of reason

and you healed him anyway

and i watched the crowd curdle like milk

as they drove us from the room i watched the boy
that no one was still watching flex and stretch the hand
that had never flexed or stretched before

and i hated him, just a little

two men, Philip and Bartholomew, came
from the marshes of the Jordan to see
you—wan ascetics, grimy from travel and
their abstemious holiness. they found us
on the beach near a bonfire. and staring at
crushed cans and sweating coolers, over
the din of the tinny radio, they said:

in prison the baptizer has heard of you
and he sends us to ask:
are you the one we have been waiting for?

and you laughed

tell the baptist what you have seen:

the blind can see
the lame can walk
the deaf can hear
the lepers are healed
the poor are fed

and the two men exchanged a glance
and stayed with us thereafter

the light i light will light the room

    nothing have i said in secret
    nothing you have said will remain so long

    every deal
    struck in your
    back halls i will
    betray from the
    rooftop
what you have done
    in the murk
i will hang like
    spotted laundry
    on the line
your careless cloying
    whisper will i
    shout for all to hear
the candle you hide
    will scorch the
    curtains and your
    sleeve
and turn your house
    to kindling

and the veil of the temple i will tear to ragged
    tatters in my teeth

until there is at last no shadow left to hide in

for behold: i have come to set a fire
and god how i wish it was already burning

can i ask you something

    almost always

      all this work. this community outreach. this feeding and this healing
             it's all very nice
             but i'm not sure what it has to do with god
    like. i get it. it's good
    but is it . . . i dunno. religion?
    i'm not saying this right maybe

oh. you think it's all vertical versus horizontal
i guess that makes sense: some guy up top
    in a nice hat and a frilly poncho and a santa claus beard
    all of this scurrying below

      that's not it
      the kingdom isn't up
then the birds would precede you
      and you are not less than birds
      the kingdom isn't down
then the whales the fish the worlds beyond would precede you
      and you are not less than they
      the kingdom isn't before
then adam would precede you
      and you are not less than he
           (sweet little muffin though he was)
      paradise is not behind. behind is only salt
        god affords to place and time no sanctity
      the kingdom is here and now
and to be in all the ages to come
    god is the making
    all verb no noun made fresh made after
    dynamic coequal coeternal consubstantial theosis
    in the kitchens and the revels and the tent
    in the ecstasy and the spheres and the work

god is love. and
love is just this:
    it is yourself
        breaking apart
        shaken to pieces
        refashioned entirely
        and made new
love is suffering for each other
god and man and life

you curl like a cat in the prow of the ship while naked sailors
quail against the mounting morning squall

because i want very much not to die wet and pantsless i grab the
carpenter joint of your shoulder and shake and you open one eye
and peer at me like a disgruntled octopus stirred from its trench
and yawn theatrically

and pop your head above the deck like a candlemas gopher and
manage the barked shout of a suburban dad annoyed by a
weekend lawn mower or garage-band teens

hey! cut it out!

and the storm stops embarrassed
and turns its head to cough

dissolving like cotton candy in a raccoon's paws
like a retreating dracula into cgi mist
and your pillow is punished with three quick jabs

                    you humans think in such
                    three-dimensional terms

          and hitting snooze on the universe

                you are back asleep

he ate always like a prince on pauper's holiday, like a
child at the fair
found lost some steps behind

winking at me as he licked lips soiled in barbecue sauce and
pointing at a flash of fire on a spittle, cultivating tummy
aches like a connoisseur at the food stalls of capernaum

peering with wide possum eyes at burbling curries and
sizzling searing chicken thighs and candying roasting
marshmallow treats that gooed his hands and stubble

belching loudly on the grass at dusk with a pile of rib
bones in styrofoam next to him as he leaned against my
shin and hooked his arm behind my other calf to loll his
head over my knee and crack his upside-down smile

while overhead the fireworks screamed and gave up the
ghost and in riot shamed the steady stalwart stars

the day was now far spent, and you had been talking for most of it. after the dunker died the crowds were larger and the threat greater and it became harder to speak in the towns, so we had come to the flat meadow delta outside bethsaida, where your voice could carry and the clover was soft under the reclining peasants and runaway slaves and curious artisans who had made the day's excursion

in the crook of the river's mouth our boat bobbed like a skittish horse, and i made sure it was rigged and ready. in my mind i saw romans swarm like a murmuration of starlings through the relaxing daytrippers, and i watched the treeline while you moved from group to group, flirting outrageously with old ladies and letting kids tackle you, ass over teakettle, like a rumpled labrador indulging rowdy puppies

i sat straddling the ship's rail, one foot dangling over the side and kicking water in an arc that didn't quite reach the prow where philip fretted

> what are we going to feed them all?

i frowned. maybe we should send everybody home. i hopped through the squish of sand and across the grass to the picnic blanket where a little boy had pinned you and was tugging on the thick locks of your hair

> we should maybe let people go home and find food

> why? there is enough

and you told the kid whose father was a baker to lend you a couple of baskets and the bit of bread and fish they had brought. and you stood and held up the baskets and said to the crowd

> take what you need and give what you can

and the baskets passed, and the people gave and took, each according to their ability and need. and in the baskets small sardines and halves of buns and figs and bright wrapped candies proliferated. and there was enough, and when it was done the baskets were full to overflowing

and from under a dog pile of five-year-olds, as a kid delivered a brutal haymaker to your stomach, you said

> behold: the miracle of the kingdom of god

balthazar, caspar, and melchior
are very pretty names but
there's really no reason to think there were even three of them
just three gifts: gold, frankincense, and myrrh
     proclaiming king and god and sacrifice
     proclaiming power and priest and corpse

terrible gifts for a baby
but then
how often we find the things we have dragged across the landscapes
of the earth are in the end
         like all art
         quite useless

The God of love my
shepherd is,
And He that doth me feed:
While He is mine, and I am
His,
What can I want or need?

He leads me to the tender grass,
Where I both feed and rest;
Then to the streams that gently
pass;
In both I have the best.

Or if I stray, He doth
convert
And bring my mind in
frame:
And all this not for my
desert,
But for His holy name.

Yea, in death's shady black abode
Well may I walk, not fear:
For Thou art with me; and Thy rod
To guide, Thy staff to bear.

Nay, Thou dost make me
sit and dine,
Ev'n in my enemies' sight:
My head with oil, my cup
with wine
Runs over day and night.

Surely Thy sweet and wondrous
love
Shall measure all my days;
And as it never shall remove,
So neither shall my praise.

—George Herbert, "The 23rd Psalm"

sometimes i am scared of forgetting the sound of you

my little guy

i'll love you forever

the rumble of your chest

the sourness of your morning breath

the way an old shirt, so misshapen on me, bulging and dipping in all the wrong places, is pulled blearily from the wardrobe and

became on you a perfect metrical sonnet

and suddenly made sense again

in toy stores or nurseries i see them among the playsets or cheerful pastel murals, safely stowed away on noah's ark, their paws on the taffrail: two little boy lions, peeking cautiously out of the masculine ruff of their proud little manes, as though they have gotten away with something and might be caught at any moment

it is not really a new phenomenon—you can spot them in paintings from even medieval masters, though there the slip endemic to the genre is aggravated by the whole "what does a lion look like" problem that beset the feudal scribal class

it is odd that this story—the apocalyptic extinction of life on earth—should become the one told to children. among the first things they learn of god is that his rage is inexhaustible. that in the porches of the sky he stores up strange horrors. best they find out young i suppose what it took me too long to understand

whenever i hear complaints about the flags rustling in the villages—you stole the rainbow it hangs in houses of sin from bodies unclean god invented it give it back—i think of those two lions. and the promise:

> in the sky i hang my bow
> that you will see, and god and life will both remember:

> there is still hope
> no matter the damage the storm has done

in any case. i keep their little stowaway cartoon secret. they might struggle to repopulate their species but something else more worthy has endured

and in this perhaps noah has been wiser than god

barracked by the clongowes well
        its steam reeking up like a fairfolk chimney
        stinking of dank moss and the heathen chemistry rites of quinta
on the lawn outside a scrubbed lancet window an unanswering sun
        goes walking through spiderwebs in thin-sock ankles
        tickled by the stubble bustling over hedgerows hardly hedgerows
        with dawn light falling on the living and the dead
        dayspring

i hear the rowdy stout thumping of the other boys in the mildewed hall
the dorm room mechanism locked behind us with a hermetic crepuscular click
        and then you: snuggling stumbling from your top pine bunk
        down, down you come a glistering phaeton
        climbing in next to me, pulling the covers over us
        your thick jock smell like a shout in my lungs

                describing our own day back to me in murmurs
                the import of brief and nameless lives
                and i am
                scared to gasp as your roving hand mid-sentence finds me and
                stays and lingers and tightens
                and swelling i find you in turn, your other hand already there
                        half-leaking as you whisper laughing

        this game is important: the t-rex cannot see us if we don't move but
        i risk a kiss on your unboxerly brow and my chin stays
        there
        with the clay of your thick unwashed curls filling my nostrils
        (but no: your head was buzzed then
                my sweet samson whose little path would make me sad) and

        we emulsify
                butting heads like stags

and you lick from your fingers hot honey tugged from the lion
i am another now and yet the same
i will be a private riddle a carcass to laugh at down the road
when
        like irish spring in the unregulated heat
        in the paddy stink and micky mud
        of the college shower's fruiting mould
                even this memory dissolves
        of you and me
           laughing in sheets

        as below, left hand pretends not to know what the right hand
        is doing

through the palace yards and courts, through the revels for the rout
of the Philistines, through the flush in their cheeks, Jonathan
brought David to his bedchamber

and Jonathan, prince of his father's house, undressed for David, and
in the bath of incensed candlelight with the clothes he shed he
covered the young shepherd

> his leather belt on David's hips
> his wooden bow in David's hand
> his thick blunt sword at David's thigh
> his gleaming plate on David's back
> his silken robe down David's belly
> his linens curled through David's loins

and the boy who was now almost unmade stood before the laughing
boy who was now both of them, and trembling in the dark promised
him the last that was left

> *thou shalt be king over Israel, and I shall be next unto thee*

> and then David and Jonathan were one

once when we were young my father with his usual weekend loutishness tumbled
down the stairs into the basement and froze mid-sentence

and you fumbled twitching jumping from the ugly futon and i have never
heard anything so loud again as your belt buckle flapping like a trout
        its clasp ringing like a cracked broken bell sounding a terrible alarm

    caught

    not:
    with your hands tangled in my hair, rough against the scalp
    pushing your length up the slick of my throat
    the apple of your cock bulging against the soft of my bruising palate
    gushing in spurts up the eager passage

    not:
    me astride you, as beneath your swollen sea-slug tuber softens spent
    and you fingered a cleft mortified red gaping tender slack with froth from
    thick skewer jackhammer piston

    but only:
    my head on your shoulder eyes half-closed
    as you traced idle circles on the flannel of my shoulder
    the gentle wooden devotion statue of some lost german master
    tucked in a snug anchorite cell
    watching tv

            your pants unfastened

    while you idly scratched at the broad hock of your thighs
    chafed by the winter cold
                    and whispered in my hair

yet for the rest of his life i felt the span of my hand press upon the force field
of this unspoken unacknowledged discovery and my father
twisting in wordlessness
at how much worse this intimacy

and i felt a white-hot brand press into my flesh and sputter there

            i was just your faggot now

be thou faithful unto death
and i will give thee a crown of life

i will give you a white stone
and on the stone a new name written

to you i shall give power over nations
to rule them with a rod of iron

and as the vessels of a potter
shall you break your foes to shivers

in Bethlehem among the shepherds a child was born

love came for him, and made of him a king

     and upon the powerful thighs of the prince
          in his hair
          across his back
     the shepherd boy of Bethlehem spilt his seed exceeding

     and David's love for Jonathan surpasseth that of women

the spirit is upon us

        to speak good news to the poor
        to heal the broken-hearted
        to free the captive
        to give sight to the blind
        to unbind the bent and bruised

        to proclaim forth a great jubilee

once your hand is on the plough
don't look back

hang on i gotta piss you announce and you grab my arm and pull
me off the log by the bonfire and plunge through parting branches
into the dark rim of woods around the beach
listening to you lashing against the leaves in a loud stream i peer
back at the distant cheerful will o' the wisp of your dorm mates
around the fire
and the distance feels the same
    why did you bring me
    i like you no i mean
and your arm reaches out to me unlooking and pulls me close your
hot breath reeks of beer and so does your piss and you kiss me
sloppily and i reach down and hold you as you finish firm and vital
like a garden hose
    still going?
    well i've got a big tank
    fuck i drank too much though
and then as you dribble to a stop and i am holding you as you shake
and you pull me backwards to the other side of the tree and push
me down into your unzipped jeans and the rich sap tobacco smell
of your perineum
i still taste the last acrid drops of urine on the tip of your dick as it
quickens and firms as you drive yourself into my mouth in rough
gagging thrusts hitting the back of my throat until my eyes are
watering and your curve is thick with my mucus and then you're
behind me, hand pushing at my jacket, and my face is against the
bark, my knees and hands in the dirt smelling the ammonia of
your piss on the other side of the tree, making a desperate
ravenous sound as you shuck off my pants and the strawberry of
your tongue jams itself into my asshole with three quick stabs and
then i feel the length of you, wet and hot and hard, rise up like a
snake to press between my buttocks, and hesitate there
    i don't want to hurt you
    and i turn to find your eyes in the dark, and i beg: hurt me
    and you do
and the fear of Isaac shoves himself suddenly inside me to the hilt

plunging brutal shaft and trunk
ancient branch of Jesse biting my neck to silence my
struggled strangle
taste the strange flesh of Sodom i have grown all my life
as salt fruit for you upon my bones
in my hand i feel the gentle beautiful stretch marks that lacerate
the tan of your backside wrinkling as you thrust into me and
soon with flesh fire inside me so terrible and torn i can feel you
about to come like a train like a tank like a mortar blast

you pull out of me frantic, and i twist, abjected, kneel before you
half-naked prostrate among the litter of fast-food containers and
crumpled receipts and broken beached condoms like jellyfish
feel you spill a white-hot newborn galaxy across my face
and then sighing take the rough club of your thumb
pushing it all in arcing scoops into my mouth
bending to kiss me, still full of your liquid communion
and in the taste of me and the taste of you and me again
i feel us blur and run

give more than you can

the disgrace of his son threw saul who was king into a fury

enmity simmered in his seething heart: to see the beautiful and popular hero
        the beloved slayer of the giant
        pinch and fondle his quivering heir like a whore
                as winks and giggles and jokes buzz in the king's ears like flies

                jonathan fallen before david the son of jesse
                        the runt of a crofter
                to his own confusion
                and the shame of his mother

        and playing upon their timbrels and tambourines the multitude sang:
                        saul has killed his thousands but
                        david has killed his tens of thousands

        david, who strums his lyre to please a fitful god
        david, who is ruddy, and of fair countenance, whose hair is sparkling
        david, who runs before the court rough southern fingers thrilling
                across the dimpled dandled back of a northern prince
                bow strung taut
                breath of the pasture
                making everywhere a song pleasing to the lord of hosts

        and in saul's grip is put a barren sceptre
                the son who should have been his staff
                now bent to chew his pillow and sheets in the rank
                sweat of an ensemened bed

                jonathan who is the prince-punk of a shepherd
                        sodomized still stinking of the lambs

        and through the riches and the wives and the music
        saul threw his spear at the darling minstrel stud

                fuck your secret chord

the next morning i am sore with flaring heat and when i squat to
shit before we drive back to the city i see in my briefs there are
drops of blood spotted there
my shameful shameless punk stigmata

and with your hand in my lap and your sleeping hair in my face in
the car
                        i happily burn

then stealing a last sandpaper kiss from you as i scramble out of
the car
i drop my duffle in the front door and peel off my jacket to go
shower upstairs and my brother points at me and says:

        oh fuck a bird got you
        good luck i guess

i pull to see the pentecostal stain and
feel myself redden
one of your thick gouts must have missed my chin
spattering a lactic constellation of you on my jacket shoulder

                        and i leave it there for days
                        so i can remember who i belong to
                        even after the scorch of my soreness recedes

until the rain in its jealousy
comes to claim it
and even that trace of you is lost to me

where is your faith?

the body is a leaky vessel

tears under a microscope speak in proteins and molecules: a tear of joy is not the tear of dust, of an onion sliced on the pink-spotted cutting board while he laughs on the couch and smiles at you and takes a photo on his phone and pulls you close to kiss your neck before he eats

when he wept as i slept his body spoke in a precise chemical composition— prolactin, adrenocorticotropic, leucine enkephalin—a briefest of verses an articulate lattice that traced the geometry of his heart breaking

if a sufficient threshold of anxiety is reached the capillaries that feed our sweat glands will burst and in the anguish in the cool of the garden while i dozed the tender flesh of his brow oozed with blood and blood will have blood by the pint by the gallon the whips and scorn of outrageous fortune lashing in signs and co-signs in the breath above the mob

and when blood loss is sufficient the body launches into hypovolemic shock the heart races the body collapses i was not there to carry his cross and to die of crucifixion is to asphyxiate is to suffocate is to put the weight of your tearing body through the legs to the iron in your wrists and feet to gasp a breath and to attempt to gulp a breath is agony is excruciating never mind to speak to

father forgive them / i promise—today, with me, you'll see paradise / god, why have you abandoned me? / please take care of my mother. be the son i wasn't. take care of each other / father i'm coming / i'm so thirsty

fluid gathers around the sac that houses the heart that houses the lungs and this pleural-pericardial effusion can rupture can burst like a bag like a dam like the porches of the heavens opened by a regretful god to loose a cataract that will drown the sorry world

it's done. it's done

carbon dioxide builds and poisons and the heart races a stress test to breakdown god gives us more than we can handle until myocardial infarction until cardiac arrest until the heart pulps and shreds itself apart

when the lance pierced his side there flowed water from the wound mixed
with blood

    he was already dead

    he died thirsty

we leave a spoor for grief to hunt

the debtor who owes five hundred and the debtor who owes fifty
shall both have their debts blotted

the labourer who begins at dawn and the labourer who begins at noon
shall both be paid a day's wage

the loyal son and the prodigal returned
shall sit together at the feast

                grace isn't just
                that is the point of grace

of course it rained in eden
        showers sweet piercing to the root
but its chiefest glory was its waterworks:
subterranean pistons pumping clear liquid light from aquifers and basins
beneath the hill of bliss
to spout and geyser freshets and cascade down
the grass-green mount of paradise's palisades:
        filling its lakes and reservoirs
        flooding terraces of dog-sweet man's cultivated rice and lilies
        flowing virtue swelling to purple the blooms of its lady's bower
everywhere refreshing the mazes and errands of her wells and rivers
enriching captive humanity's wilderness enclosure
as busy adam delved and busied eve spun

        when the world fell
        when rash hand in evil hour plucked and ate
        when cherubic fires scorched its briars and its fields to ash

cruel hands ancient before time pulled the rock of eden from the earth like a
tooth
lifted it above the scudding scouring clouds
and dropped it from a height within the sea
an ungainly unholy asteroid an orbital bombardment to smite the stegosaur
and flat the gulf
        to teach thee: that god attributes to place no sanctity
        to sentiment no countenance
        and show you this is how he treats his friends

there haphazard the
broken ceramic engine of the isle sputters and clogs at unwholesome angle
its drills and casings putrefied in malfunction but faltered haltered chugging
on
the mechanic fallen angel heart the cracked hydraulic of eden's omphalos
      still pumps and swells
            foaming fouling fountains from below
      to poison gulls and pollute the sound
      to choke a swollen river mouth in thick
          and oily wormwood
          from the seabed's rotten petrol heart

          and aboard a rotten carcass
          not rigged, nor tackle, sail, nor mast

          i reached its inked and stinking margins

          and by rites and right of exile

          of wretched eve and mother sycorax
i claimed this island mine

don't pray in public

those that do
            have already got what they wanted out of it

        and it had nothing to do with god

after this i looked, and behold, a door was opened in heaven
and a voice as a trumpet said: come up hither
and see what must be hereafter

and behold, a throne was set in heaven
and one sat upon the throne

and he was like jasper and sardonyx and emerald
and an iris crested round his throne

and round the throne were four and twenty seats
with four and twenty elders sitting clothed in white
and on their heads were crowns of gold

and amidst the thunder and the lightning were seven lamps of fire
and before it was a sea of glass

and four beasts:
a lion
a calf
a man
an eagle

with six wings and full of eyes cried out

HOLY, HOLY, HOLY LORD GOD ALMIGHTY
who was, and is, and is to come

and at his feet the elders fell and cast their golden crowns

beware for me, my brothers
beware for me, the children of Rome
that they affix to their walls

beware for me, my friends
who are like the transept of the cross
and worship in the crucifix

beware for me, my brothers
for if a carpenter can fashion a god

the god fashioned by a carpenter!
then who fashioned the carpenter?

and life is praised

and life triumphs!

—The Book of the Baptist

the whole world goes into its grave

when even hope exhausts
even despair has its faithfulness
holding on to life long enough for grace to find it

     let me only say something
     worth the saying
          let me only do something
          worth the doing

if you could see the way out
it wouldn't be much of a miracle

in 1400 years of depictions of saint christopher his face always
registers an annoyed fuck this little bastard
as the child who is the word and world wriggles into piggyback
tugging on his hair and otherwise ruining his goddamn life

this hairy mammoth werewolf of a man whom you tease and
domesticate
this ursine babysitter you menace like a brat

god playing with his gay uncle

every time i see him in oils and icons fording a river with you
dandled on his broad back rolling his eyes as you kick him
in the ribs i remember:

you pushing my cousins a little too hard on a tire swing or
letting one wriggle past you with a soccer ball at camping,
wiping yourself out theatrically while she scored a goal. your
knees filthy for the rest of the night

or when i woke at your mother's house to find you had spent
the morning shovelling the driveway with the neighbour kids
making a snowman, whose huge white frozen ass was now
mooning me at the door

kids get it
ask for what you want and expect it
feel deeply
that's what the world should be

now i catch you in museums and cathedrals dandled in your mother's
arms holding a pomegranate you slobber with toothless gums or sneaking
gifts to german children and wonder what it must be like:

to grow young again
a two-thousand-year-old baby
yelling "again" at the sunrise

rejoice! for
prophets kings and ages

have longed to see
what you have seen
and did not see

have longed to hear
what you have heard
and did not hear

near the brook under a disinfectant sun our clothes lay nursing their wounds, tender from the agonies of cleanliness we had inflicted on them

the magdalene had broken pellets of her expensive nard in the town's old stone basins like oily rainbows on its surface along with some sachets of half-dried lavender stubs and spiderwort. the perfume hung sweetly atop the sharp tang of the fuller's vat where she and i had both giggled as we donated our own warm micturition to the drum where our underwear soaked bleaching. now while they dried we rinsed ourselves in the thick trickling downstream lather of the wash, dousing away the dust and heat of the road

i took a handful of the sudsing foam from the basin and pushed it through my hair, cold water rivulets cresting round my neck and down my chest. up in the cliffs let them yell and debate the nature of the godhead; here nestled in the gully's cool stones, away from the town and the jock jostle of the other disciples and the scrutiny of strangers, i felt her whole manner unkinking and uncoiling with her hair, whose complicated tresses she was unknotting in the stream

the wide stretch of her ferocity and inquiry bought me a space for my quiet watching that is, i suppose, the usual shade afforded every boy like me who gravitates to the aunts' table at the family party. when the others fell to baffled silence she demanded, counter-claimed, debated. when you broke my heart as you did often she listened, and telegraphed a goggling smirk on mornings when she clocked me wobbling

"god look at you. you're disgusting," she sighed, theatrically puffing a ringlet from her own forehead, smacking a streak of dirt from my thigh, raising a bright red welt with the hand towel as she scrubbed and i squealed like a piglet delighted to be babied

        they said after you were gone she went mad—dwelling in
      wastes, covered in pelts and dirt, brooding on mortality. i doubted it.
      amid the collectivist rumpus of the others she made me less ashamed
      of my own fussiness. graceful and present, she made of herself a
      prayer and she would not have flung away the dignity she had fought
      for, though i know why so many would delight at the fantasy

then again the elastic of me has broken and stretched so much that i doubt
she would recognize much of the shy lost boy she wendied. and i would
begrudge no one the balsam balm of their madness

> but she was not a woman easily broken

i miss her, sometimes, as much as i miss you

suddenly andrew came hurtling through the bush. she dodged at his
intrusion but the whites of his eyes were too panicked to rove

> they're going to kill him

in the panic the half-wet laundry we rummaged onto ourselves was cool
and bright against our skin as we flew up the hill and saw the mob trying
to beetle you over the cliff face. we tried to push through, to put something
soft between the crowd and you, when i felt a hand slip into mine

> what are you looking for?

> i jammed a kiss that was half a head-butt into your face and we
> hustled you away from the throbbing lemmings. she was less
> relieved and scoured you like a pan with reprimands about what
> you had done and how you had gotten out

> the usual things. extruding rich people through camels' eyes, laws
> are stupid. you know

oh god. how did you escape

oh that. well
> space-time folds like linen
> like laundry on the line
and the raiment of this body we can doff we can shed like a snake like a
sindon slipping in a soldier's clutch

> oh
> ok
> > i guess

you smiled your crooked smile smushed your face into a wink and pressed your nose into my scalp

surviving is easy

it's the other thing that's hard

you smell nice

and we headed back to the shady gully, to fetch our forgotten underwear and rinse the crowd out of your face and hair

who hath ascended up into heaven
or descended?

who hath gathered the wind
in his fists?

who hath bound the oceans
in his garment?

who hath established all
the ends of the earth?

       what is his name, and what
       is his son's name

       if thou canst tell?

with palm fronds waving they met you upon your donkey
upon the foal of a donkey

the sweet beast anxiously braying as he picked his way gingerly
through the stones of the eastern gate
watching the children trumpeting, blowing quacks through reeds
as we climbed the zigzag rise to the majestic city of god's footstool

and you beheld it rising in all its might and grandeur and you said
to the crowd:

> do you see all these great buildings?
> someday not a stone will stand atop another
> every one will be thrown down
>
> nothing is housed in churches and temples and holy places
> that is not housed in you

leave me limping
sodomite son of a sodomite david
god born in a sty
laid in a manger to be food for all the world
milk me with the rough stable hands of a carpenter shepherd
shudder your praise into my shoulder like a ram
as naked man with naked man contends
like jacob and his angel
and let my salvation be worked out
   in field and pasture
   in fear and trembling
   in seed spilled upon the stone

why do you fear
those who can only kill your body
and after this are powerless?

there was a theological position, prevalent since the early centuries then recurring throughout medieval thought both orthodox and heretical, that because your humours must have been perfectly balanced—because your diet was an isomorphic index to your virtue—therefore you had perfectly harmonious digestion

and consequently never pooped

this doctrine was devised by someone who had never been viciously trapped in the blanket of yet another of your earth-rank morning dutch ovens
shushing me in chuckles through the sheet in case Peter's mother-in-law heard
and pealing with laughter at my tussle against soft linen and strong arms

indeed whole wings of gnostic sects would tumble and fall
to the mortifying regret of the serene heretic Valentinus and church father Clement of Alexandria and medieval monk Epiphanius and with him all the Docetists of old if they had seen you:

grunting out a thick shit on the toilet in the morning, the bathroom door forgotten open, half-singing a song you had made up yourself, shouting at me to check this out which i suppose to Valentinus's accommodated relief i at least never did, leaving the historical and theological record a gap of decency

and then you would saunter back with a *whew*, daubing your brow in broad pantomime with the crook of your elbow-sleeve and then tackling me on the couch, kissing me wolfishly as though somehow perversely invigorated by your disburdening like a drunk frat boy suddenly horny again after a good vomit did i ever tell you about the night i was born?

yes many times. none of them reconcilable
the star. the manger. the shepherds. the wise men

the little kid shitting his pants in the corner

the what

oh yeah. i think he came with the shepherds? i dunno
poor little bastard

he crawls into the barn with the rest of the shepherds
in awe at the ineffable incarnation and so on
but
he's really gotta go, you know
so he pops a squat in the corner and just takes a massive embarrassed
dump
in front of everyone like: the virgin mother, the sheep, the angel. the
whole deal
which unfortunately
delighted the infant me

of course

of course
so then after that whenever he pooped it came out as delicious candy
you know
as a blessing

is that . . . a blessing?

well
(ok so this next part's not my fault but)
unfortunately
the local children eventually caught wind of this (so to speak)
and took to chasing him around the village beating him mercilessly
with sticks

till he crapped out more candy
so i guess long run not so much a
blessing really

this is how you treat your friends

you never heard of the pooping nativity scene guy?
i think he turned into like a candy log
a pinata situation
you know

so is that a different kid than the drum kid?

> fuck. it's not my place to judge
> (i mean sometimes it is)
> but who plays a drum at a newborn baby
>
> like i would beg you to read the room
> swaddled infant king aside the lady just gave birth
> please cut her some slack

should have turned *him* into a pooping candy log

you move, as ever, in mysterious ways
geez turn on the fucking fan

somewhere
even the hairs of your head
have been counted

a kingdom divided will come to desolation
a house divided will fall

    and so beware:
    your enemy in Hell is well-organized
    and well-administered

    the whole town had grown claustrophobic—too small, and too close
to the people who had known you all your life—who remembered a boy
crying over a broken toy or marching behind the bier of the dead old man
he had called his father

    wasn't this
    the bastard of a cuckolded old fool
    who they tricked into wedding a girl already pregnant

    can anything good come from nazareth?

    prophets are never welcome home

when i was young my grandmother would tell a joke:

a woman had three sons, handsome and strong. but a fortune
teller warned her:

> one shall be a beggar
> one shall be a thief
> one shall be a murderer

and the woman was horrified, but she was also sensible. and so
she raised them, one by one:

> one to be a priest
> one to be a banker
> one to be a cop

> i don't think you ever met her, but i think you
> would have liked her

> she liked you

life is more than meat
and the body more than raiment

    the ravens do not keep a barn
    but god feeds them

    the lilies do not spin or sew
    but god dresses them in majesty

can you worry yourself taller?
or keep at bay the white of your hair?

fear not
and keep your faith
in what the thief cannot reach
and the moth cannot gnaw

capernaum was a cheerful tugboat polyp on the upper lip of the sea of galilee

a "sea" in which i grew like a reed half-submerged was really a freshwater lake,
fed from the north by the pump of the jordan's aorta as it cascades towards
the south, the waters of the upper plateau and valley coalescing from little
brooks to cataracts
      multiplying one fish to thousands
from a small leaky dinghy to the sweaty seagull-squawk bustle of my
father's fleet pulling wriggling flitting schools from its shy little shallows to
build a town and a proud little empire he thought to leave to his ungrateful
and unfaithful sons

when the earth was young all of this had been a vast lagoon of water on the
wine-dark mediterranean, but as the world's heart hardened and its arteries
calcified and shrank the crust pinched and tightened, and the west bank
pulled itself east, folding itself into the history of men, into the stamp of
the hellenic and hasmonean, and it forgot the way back to the oceans

and all the troops of babylon and assyria and parthia and rome swarmed
like beetles across its earth

      and their gods buzzed like locusts over the fields
      haunting grove with timbrelled anthem
      braiding hungry thirsty roots into the rock of judah
      raising idols in dismal dance above the furnace maw

                i have abandoned the conviction of my father
                apostate in your arms
                a body profaned and torn

and now below galilee this trickle of water abandons gaulanitis and the
chirp of capernaum and bethsaida to fall southwards
      its current become a swift rocky cascade
         and plummets deep below the limits of the oceans to the
dead sea—
with nowhere now to go, its churn is choked, evaporating in a cruel
alkaline sun, and leaves its briny rim for reddened tourists to float
         and life to wither in
         here stood sodom rising in her heights
         figures frozen shambling in strange images of death

even as children we knew that south, towards the city
                              death was waiting
                              seething in the brackish mud

          and i
          looking back
          am struck to stalag salt

i send you into this world as a lamb among wolves

and so:

be innocent as the dove

and cunning as the adder fanged

in 1959 in central Lisbon
the cathedral of Sao Domingos is destroyed by fire

it is reopened in 1994 but left by the Portuguese
half-ruined and disfigured: melted
charred
patchwork left obvious
like an acid victim whose face a drunk God has smote
to teach some brutal, incoherent lesson

      it still smells
      in the coolness of the night
      like smoke

   resurrection leaves its scars

after they killed you and smote the temple and sunk a place for
wailing like a gravity-well upon the earth, the Romans washed
upriver chasing renegades from the smoulder

bringing brine in their wake / to wash the brackish bank

and they found our little village and the sea on which it lay, and with
the fawning simper of all conquistadors renamed it Tiberias—another
laurel to festoon their emperor

> i doubt, recumbent upon his treasure pleasure island amid
> the honeyed tangle of Capri's pliant and oily youths, rosebud
> assholes perfect pink and perfumed, that the pot-bellied
> god-king Caesar noticed much

> nor in Rome was hard-bit Sejanus like to have spared a
> second frown

and doubtful most of all that the laughing little lake with its pulsing
nursemaid minnows felt the lash of churlish vandalism as another little
king set his throne on the beach and bid still the waves

whatever waterbucket boys play on the shore do not diminish its might
and *messieurs believe me there is no way of turning the tide*: god may laugh in
flowers but in the waters i have heard his roar his rage and there have seen
his foot upon the treadle of the loom

> in the beginning was the fence and

> there is no one left who can tame the sea

but now i squat like a shag like a scamel like a crab going backwards
on my own crag salt and bare
too much of water and too much of stone
> the haunt of seals and orcs and sea-mews' clang

> and i find too late you bent my slow tongue to word incarnate
> and split my lip with ember char
> only so that i might know
> > how to curse

no
            the bright day is done and i
        am for the dark

i am mrs danvers tugging at lace, in galleries where walls continue upright
        bricks meet neatly
        floors firm
        doors sensibly shut
        twirling amid gas-can curtains i sometimes wonder when i feel my
mind clench like a fist what it might have been, instead:

        to have started from dozing in my chair and squinted to see the
        shuffling hedgehog of red crests and dulling spears coming over the hill

        and to have clucked my tongue

to have the pleasure of the prickly grief of knowing where they laid my
father wrapped in linen
        and to have sung a tattered kaddish for him
and been glad he did not live to see the soldiers spit in capernaum's streets
and piss like steaming horses against the wall where he whispered a young
love song to my mother

to have had a sturdy wife grow a little ugly with me, and slightly stupid
children to be my comfort, to watch women come and go talking of
michelangelo and leonardo and donatello and raphael and young men
come a-courting nieces and granddaughters whose names i dimly
remember but whose joys and whose features character my own

look, there, on the blushing bride—the swoop of my brow that you never fell
in love with, the curl of my lip that you never kissed—instead imprinted on
a dozen faces crowding around a table of gibes of merriments gambols
and songs

        and i the fool—surfeit-swelled, so old and profane—at times
ridiculous, wont to set the table on a roar

what it might have been if time and tide had been gentle, if the water
could roll back: to have felt history glide by me as carelessly and cool as
the jordan while lords liars and lunatics waded and splashed and bid
bored armies march a baptism

to live, and pray, and sing, and tell old tales, and laugh at gilded butterflies, and

to declare, to no one at all, when soldiers arrive (as they always arrive) a hulking twisted Guernica, with the car window rolled down passport and postcard in hand and with the privilege of the old and the soft that *it was not so when i was young,* and

    it's a shame

        what a shame

to have been a little bit silly, and a little bit pitied, and a little bit loved

        but my way of life
    is fall'n into the sear, the yellow leaf;
    and that which should accompany old age,
    as honour, love, obedience, troops of friends,
    i must not look to have

    trees that do not flourish are cast in the fire

        let the dead bury their dead

and the rectum is a grave

so i dine on locusts and honey, and wear regret like a cardigan that is as forgetful of my shape as i am, and enter rooms it seems sometimes you have just slipped out of, and keep no lighthouse

i am ever so much more than twenty. i grew up long ago
    i promised not to
        i couldn't help it

    and in the mirror everyday i watch busy death set about its work
        like bees in a hive of glass

living in terror of the shadow at the nursery window, cringing from a touch that would burst me like a balloon like an old skin filled with new wine if you felt for furrows ploughed on a face when more than forty winters have besieged my brow and dug deep trenches in beauty's field

my king. my jove. i speak to thee my heart

and i the old cat man crouching with his books in the dust of the senate, lying that the cracks do not hurt (the naming of cats is a difficult matter) while Francis #7 gives chase and the blessed saints ascend to Carousel

Anon, Francis? No, Francis; but tomorrow, Francis;
or, Francis, o' Thursday; or indeed, Francis, when
thou wilt. But, Francis!

renew! renew! renew!

the sun rises every morning i do not rise every morning but the variation is due not to my activity but to my inaction it might be true that the sun rises regularly because he never gets tired of rising his routine might be due not to a lifelessness but to a rush of life a child kicks his legs rhythmically through excess not absence of life because children have abounding vitality because they are in spirit fierce and free therefore they want things repeated and unchanged they always say do it again and the grown-up person does it again until he is nearly dead but perhaps god is strong enough to exult in monotony it is possible that god says every morning do it again to the sun and every evening do it again to the moon it may not be automatic necessity that makes all daisies alike it may be that god makes every daisy separately but has never got tired of making them it may be that he has the eternal appetite of infancy for we have sinned and grown old and our father is younger than we

and thus it will go on, so long as children and gods are gay
and innocent and heartless

    and the ashes blow towards us with the salt wind
from the sea

    and i try to remember:

        what did i go out into the desert to find?

blessed are those who
go hungry
      so the stomach of another
      is filled

on the saturday i return to the potter's field and find the crumpled wet
leftovers of the naked traitor burst like a butcher's groceries in a thick
smear across the rock beneath the tree

    and through the ugly mass of stinging stable flies i slowly dig
    him a sandy hole. not much of one, as i have only my sissy hands
    and i do not think my heart is much in it and it seems unfair to
    deny the buzzards the meal they have already begun in stringy
    gnaws of his cock and eyes and nose

    but if they want to redeem any of him from the earth they will
    have to work for it

    i suppose that's how it always goes

and i nudge him in with my foot and he tumbles and i kick the dirt back
over him mingled with his shower of blood-muddled coins. it was hot
work and it was not worth it

i try to find a prayer but it catches in my gorge and i
finally vomit in a tidy splash like a cat. fit monument for
both of us. maybe it is poison leaving my system. i have
always metabolized poison well

he was what he was. i do not have much pity for him,
even with his guts unseamed and his cheek eaten. he will
be exhumed many times over—by the birds, by the
scholars, by sullen teens and pop stars

    only in this do i have any sympathy:

    i know how horrible it is to have history notice you out of the
    corner of its eye

        let the clay steal the clay and
        the dead bury the dead

Almighty and most merciful Father:

> We have erred, and strayed from Thy ways like lost sheep.
> We have followed too much the devices and desires of our
> own hearts. We have offended against Thy holy laws.
> We have left undone those things which we ought to have
> done; And we have done those things which we ought not to
> have done.
>
> And there is no health in us.
>
> But Thou, O Lord, have mercy upon us, miserable offenders.
> Spare Thou those, O God, who confess their faults.
> Restore Thou those who are penitent; According to Thy
> promises declared unto mankind in Christ our Lord.
>
> And grant, O most merciful Father, for His sake; That we
> may hereafter live a godly, righteous, and sober life, To the
> glory of Thy holy Name.
>
> Amen.
>
> —The Book of Common Prayer

to be rich
is to be damned

your weight pushing down hard impossible and through my
relenting flesh, and i am suffocant stinging dissolved ripped apart
by each thrust into the white-hot obliterated

you drop with a groan
your heft lands upon my left hand and
my mind swims back reluctant through muffled ear thrum warm,
and slippery you pull me tight to yourself soft softening

a heap of fur and arms and legs a paw rough and big that cups
against the hair that coats my belly and tangles itself there thick
and tacky before tracing upwards slicing me unseamed shivering
in two through the down to my breastbone and you blow night air
damp skin cool in a cascade shiver

> the chill breath of a mule against me dozing
> Peace

i twist. Even in the dim your eyes. Behind you the faintest
mutters of firelight play on polyester, shadows indistinct and
alien swelling and deflating as the tent's skin ripples in the hot
night. Outside are shapes like trees, walking. Headlights flare
suddenly against the canvas, drunkenly hailed by the slumped
forms chestnuts roasting beside the fire as beneath its wheels,
the crumpled rattle of perforated cans rake broken, martyred tin
bodies across sharp stones

Watching you I listen. Water slides unblinking through sweat
from the edge of my eye into the hollow of my ear; I move to
wipe it, but you lap the tear from the porch of my ear with your
small, warm tongue. I inhale sharply, forgetful of staring lights,
ecstatic at feeling you again threatening, again unlatching and
unravelling and unfastening me as you coat the whorls of my
earlobe with electric molasses. But you press closer and make a
sound like laughing

Always crying, I feel you sigh gently into my shoulder. I jab your
side with my elbow, instantly afraid you will pull away in
exaggerated passion, leaving me exposed and unmoored, but

you squeeze more tightly, throwing your long leg with its flat, wide foot over my waist, holding my cock in the small of your knee. Your warm, sour breath on my nape mingles with the stale heat of the tent and the musk of you and the acrid olive trees

i am
who you say
i am

we walk the road to Jericho. the wind is rubbing against the
hoarse grain sea, blond and scratching petulant at the rudeness
of the morning. you are talking animatedly with the murmur,
but i am listening to the chubby sparrows speaking Greek amidst
the dust, the rules of their game incoherent and boisterous

as they take off my eye catches yours; you wink, and the flesh
around my spine freezes like a tongue to iron

i am
who i say
i am

a bearded lady hangs upon a cross

      a beautiful virgin to whom god sent a thick bushy beard
      to preserve her chastity
      because her father would have her wed a pagan

      because they were too ashamed to show you hanging naked
      afraid of the body you gave up
      afraid of what it would mean
      to consider truly and honestly the flesh of god

      so they painted you clothed
      crucified in flowing robes of brocade and scarlet

      and others gazing in confusion
      made up a story to explain
      this beautiful hairy figure in a dress

      a misunderstanding
      as most saints are

saint wilgefortis did not exist

      saint wilgefortis
      maiden martyr
      genderfuck daughter of god
            pray for us

the soldier kneels. his armour is glittering in the hot sun that still
cuts aslant through the porticoes of the courtyard. the muscles of
his chestplate carefully sculpted, its nipples and navel lovingly
rendered by some distant, appreciative faggot artisan and then
pressed en masse across the sea in a smoking roman forge

he is, like his panoply, extraordinarily beautiful: calves and haunches
thickened by military drills beneath his short skirt, threatening to
burst the brown cerements of his high sandals, arms veined from a
thousand training spear-thrusts, brown hair cropped short, clean-cut
jaw stubbling from the last few days of worry

he has spent his deployment breaking and killing us

i wonder how young he was when they sent him here smelling of italy's
boot. was he poor or rich, ambitious or hopeless, when he came and saw
and conquered another barbarous bleating horde

he looks uncomfortable
he is girt with a heavy twilled scarlet robe. it would be impressive as finery
in procession and doubtless a warm blanket on the field, but it clearly
now encumbers and smothers him. roman armour was not designed for
levantine heat, was not designed to kneel
and as he sweats in thick lubricious beads from the oven of his leather and
bronze casing and the press of the hostile crowd finally he speaks to you

    sir
    i do not know your god, nor you
    i have not had much use for gods of any kind

        i have followed orders and given them
        and i know power collects and pools and calls itself a god
        and it might as well be, so long as power lasts

    but the man i love is dying
    and i will kneel to whatever spirit or man or devil can save him

    i am not worthy. i don't care about worthiness
    but only say the word, that he can be healed

and to my left i smell the breath of iscariot rise in high-pitched keen:
     some traitor twink greases wide his cunt for colonizer cock
     and now lies dying from some trench-grown syphilis?
     good
     one less camp-slut for rome
     one less fanboy gumming on power's prick
        let him choke on it

cheeks hot i find my gaze connect with his eyes already on me

     and i understand what he sees:
     just a darling plaything for his master
     a cheap indulgence on the road
        whose discard he will savour

     i wish his tongue would shrivel to the root and fall out
you look at the traitor, then look at me, and decide to skip it

instead you crouch to touch and smooth the centurion's dripping hair

        god is love
        not power

            go and find them well
            you have made them so
            not me

and the soldier stands
and nods
flexes and shakes his thick-roped legs
     and curtly bows and walks away

the lord is hard
       he reaps where he has not sown
       and gathers where he has not
       scattered seed

       and we know neither the day nor hour
          when he comes

when i frowned in perplexity at some abstruse point of
doctrine, jamming the question-quills from my mane into
my mother's thighs, she used to tell a story:

once upon a time, an old man sat upon the seashore

and wondered how it was: that three could be one, and one could be three,
that a man could be god, or god a man
why we suffer, why we fell

how many angels might dance upon the head of a pin

who is the third who walks alongside
drinking liquor and tasting wine and not blood

who is the fourth who stands in the fire
and is not consumed

and as the old man furrowed, folding and wheezing like an attic accordion,
on shoes and ships and sealing-wax and cabbages and kings
ruminating the cud of allusions and delusions that a minute might reverse

he saw a boy upon the beach

skipping from wave to sand and back, dumping a bright green pail of water
into a hole he had dug into the dunes

and the old man asked: what are you doing?

and the boy replied:

i am moving the ocean

and the old man scoffed, and he said:

this you can never do. the hole is too small, and the ocean too vast
and the sea is wet as wet can be, and the sands as dry as dry

and the boy said:

sooner will i do this, than you will find your answer

and he was gone

The Vision of the Heretic Julian of Norwich
from the Middle English

He shewed me a little thing, the
quantity of an hazel-nut, in the palm of
my hand, and it was as round as a ball.
I looked thereupon with the eye of my
understanding, and thought: What may
this be? And he answered thus: It is all
that is made.

I marvelled how it might last, for
methought it might suddenly have
fallen to naught, for little.

And I was answered in my
understanding: It lasteth, and ever
shall, because it is loved.

Then he looked at me and he said this
word: Thou shalt not be overcome. Full
clearly and full mightily, with full
assuredness and comfort against all
tribulations that may come.

He said not that: Thou shalt not be
tempested, thou shalt not be travailed,
thou shalt not be afflicted; but He said:
Thou shalt not be overcome.

I know there is sin in the world,
but all shall be well, and all shall
be well, and all manner of thing
shall be well.

to whom much is given
much shall be
required

they say he will return one day

        spinning in the engine of his great iron centrifuge
            with the ox the lion the eagle and the man
                wearing the old bruised-flesh
          scarecrow out of storage
              a smile nailed to his face and
          neat, tight incision scars of excellent work
          beneath his chin

        stripping the paint of the world in blistering sheets
        come again to judge the living and the dead

        behold: an artificial adam crashing down at megiddo,
        paving gehenna to put up a depraved parking-lot paradise

          and no sooner said but a
     vast image troubles my sight:

and i saw a new heaven and a new earth,
        for the first heaven and the first earth are passed away

        and the sea
              where i foamed for you like a mermaid
              where i was your selkie boy, spent in spume
              where my name was written in water
        shall be no more

maybe by then i won't be here anymore

i will have slipped out
        past the party lights and pantheons remote
        shrouded in a cloak of mushroom

           homeward returning

                        maybe i will
                        let you
                        wait for me this time

i wake like proust madeleine crumbs in a bed
whose coordinates are unclear. the ballast shifts
and i remember who i am but not where this is. it
hurts to live

i think they broke your arm

she is sitting perched on a stool, her face resting on her knee, the
wanton ringlets of her tresses gripped in the forgivenessless teeth
of a plastic clamshell clip. her toenails are a pretty pink

what did you say to them that they beat you so bad

god is love

well that explains it
the big fella your brother i guess went to get your boss

where am i?

you're in my father's house. one of them
no one comes to fishgut little galilee except the passing garrisons so.
he keeps his little secrets here. plus the beach is good for his skin

i look around. the bed is flung with a bright crochet of pastel squares whose
weight snugly smothers me. the room is expensive, its walls plastered and
smooth in the new roman style. a small vanity with beautiful movie-star
light bulbs all around it is littered with a riot of lipsticks and big pretty
bottles of perfume, and under the photos tucked in its mirrorglass, a
dented roman helmet rests askew on a styrofoam head decked in full
crooked mascara and false lashes. above all this, from the antlers of a colossal
and delicate deer skull, bleached from the desert, dangle a hundred glittering
necklaces and pendants, catching and sprinkling little patches of coloured
fairy light. outside the big window is too much sunlight and the sea

who
                i am the witch of magdala
                the perfumed whore of the tents of rome
                she who commands the seven devils

she turns a wiggling finger in a circle in the air, woggling her eyebrows, and then cracks her back as she stretches from her long slump on the chair

> we found your brother, holding you all broken on the street. sounds like things got nasty

i suddenly remember the close punch that found my ribs, and pull back the blanket to find a bright purple blotch spreading there

> yeah some of those are broken too i think. you must have really pissed them off

i manage a grimace. at least the colours are neat. i've never been in a proper fight before. does a beating count as a fight

> you're with that saviour kid
> he fucks you right

it isn't a question

> please i know another bottom when i see one

i feel my forehead get hot. she moves to wipe my brow as it beads, and the cloth is cool and smells like peppermint and something bleats in pain on my forehead like a quail's egg

> i guess we both like the feel of power's dick

> though in these unprecedented times i prefer mine uncut
> they have more money and you need less lube

she smiles at me winking

> but maybe you like it a little rough on the way in

even as i feel myself flushing i can tell she is enjoying trying to shock me. i don't know what it means that part of me thrills at it. at least it isn't peter turning embarrassed when i rest my head against your shoulder

> thanks

> it's fine. apparently he healed me once. your top. we haven't met but maybe i owed him

something crosses her face, drawing her eyes to the window and is
gone. she stands to draw a sheer across the drape runner dimming
the room so i can sleep

> well he can do his woo-woo thing and kiss it better when he gets here
> if he wants but i think i did a pretty good job
> it's a bad bump but no concussion

if you need anything just holler. dad is out of town but my sister martha
is outside too. she sucks but she's ok

you're very cute. i'm sure he'll be here soon

once in my cousin's basement my brother
and i were playing knights
this consisted mostly of holding the
hideous cushion roundels of my aunt's
couch to use as shields and unscrewing the
legs of the ottoman to wield as swords and
shouting at each other

it was tremendously fun
until the wooden leg flew from his hand and struck me in the forehead

and i screamed and gushed blood and sat crying pitiably on the
bathroom sink while my mother and aunts cooed and clucked at the gore
and my brother bawled desperate apologies and hid in the concrete cellar

my brother died in Jerusalem
his head struck from his body by order of Herod

the scar should be all i have left of him
but when i touch my forehead it is not there
and i wonder if perhaps i am remembering wrong
and it was me who threw the chair-leg
and he who bled for it

the poor always get
poorer

when i was a child we were in the sacristy pulling our white robes over our tracksuits and tennis shoes to serve a mass when we saw a bat asleep in the sink

the church was very cold and very old and the pipes kept heat. the little guy must have cozied to the porcelain and drowsed into a stupor when the sun rose like a tiny dracula

and the other boy, who was the worst, said

    let's burn it

and flicked the butane lighter off and on

and behind me i felt a presence and turned to meet the parish's new priest: massy and young and acerbic and he said

    i can tell you're going to be the one that's a problem

and as the other boy scurried away i watched awestruck as he scooped the little bat up in his hands and casually walked him up the ladder into the belfry and half-tossed him into an aerial zigzag into its upper reaches and it sprung into being like a clay bird clapped to life

and back near the altar he handed me a box of wooden matches (because the other boy, who was hiding, still had the lighter) and told me to light the candles and i confessed i didn't know how to light matches and he said

    it's like the bat
    it'll only hurt you if you're afraid of it

and he struck one off the altar stone and handed me the flame

grant me
the joy of being one with you

i reject the multiplicity of creatures
master
i want nothing
          but unity with you
you master
are enough for me
in you master
is all i need

true friend of my heart
unite my soul poor and alone
to your great singularity

you are all mine master
when can i say
that i am all yours?

the magnet pulls the iron
and grasps it to itself
          pull me
          grasp me
          clasp me
          press me

fuse my heart forever to your fatherly chest

if i was created for you
why do i not dwell with you?

engulf me
in the abyss of your goodness

if you love me
why not force me
          as i really want?

                    —saint francis de sales

i will turn child against parent
and parent against child

        and i bring not peace
        but gunfire

you are already dead when they pierce your side

when they hang you up above the altars in the basilicas and cathedrals
and chapels and kitchens in bad bernini knockoffs it's not a man
suffering in extremis. it's just a corpse just a mangle for the dogs.
whatever was the thing of you was gone
       it didn't hurt. you were already dead
       no one even noticed

we watch from the bottom. i hold your mother. i stink of
another man's piss but what can she possibly care. i
don't. we are the indexes of you the bodies you touched
and entered and passed through oh god that man should
be a thing for immortal souls to sieve through numinous
beings sluiced through hamburger meat
she can barely stand and i want to rush the pole where
you are dying and let them quill me with spears like a
dog swollen by a porcupine if i can just die holding you if
there can be no moment i wasn't no measure of it every
second i am not touching you is a betrayal so much
worse than his

at least he got to kiss you goodbye. at least he knew it was the last one
i am already forgetting

      please take care of my mom
      please take care of each other
      this is your son now this is your mom now
      oh god

      a coming out a wedding in post-mortem she is crying
and i wish she wouldn't look she keeps looking and i get my
wish but. soon the soldier puts his spear through your side
and it slides in resistless like a skewer like the barb of a
thermometer through a finished roast. blood and water you
were already
i wasn't watching when you
now there is just meat getting cold
      when god died he died whimpering

longinus is by convention his name
the soldier
he is supposed to realize like lightning, an electric current passing
through, that he has been complicit in a great crime. "surely this must be
the son of god," he's supposed to say as the skies glower and darken and
the graves yield up their sleepers

and, disgusted with himself, he is supposed to walk away from a life
of inflicting the cruel will of the powerful against the righteous
shedding the heavy plates of his armour into the sand like scales

and people go after the lance for centuries
the spear of destiny
not grasping it's the weapon you're supposed to leave behind
in the dust
they seek for the living among the dead

longinus just means "spear"
it's not really a name
a soldier refusing to serve injustice would be a miracle wouldn't it

i didn't see a miracle. just a dead thing
a maker unmade

for the strength to walk away
saint longinus pray for us

psalm 109

hold not thy peace, o god of my praise
for the mouths of the wicked and the mouths of the deceitful are
opened: they have spoken against me with a lying tongue
i am compassed about with words of hatred and fought against
without cause
my friendship they meet with contempt
my good they reward with evil, and hatred repays my love
and thus i give myself unto prayer

so:
set thou a foe against my enemy. let satan stand at his right hand
when he shall be judged, let him be condemned. let his prayer fall
dead at his feet and condemn him
let his days be few; let another take his office
let his children be orphans; leave his wife a widow
let his progeny be vagabonds and beggars, driven from the ruin of
their homes to seek their bread amid the desolation

let the thief and the moth catch all that he hath; let the stranger
spoil and plunder his work
let there be none to extend mercy unto him, none to show him
kindness, none to pity his fatherless brood
let his posterity be cut off, and their name blotted out
let the iniquity of his fathers be remembered, and let not the sin of
his mother be forgotten
let god remember them all, so that the world forgets

for he never dreamt of doing a kindness
but hounded to death the poor, the needy, and the broken-
hearted
for he loved to pronounce a curse
so let it come back to him
for he delighted not in blessing
so let it be far from him

as he clothed himself with cursing like as with his garment, so let it
seep into his bowels like water
       like oil into his bones
   let it be like a cloak shrouded around him, and a belt girded tight
to bind him

   help me, god
       for i am bereft
       and my heart is broken
       and in the dust this is all the prayer i know

i am sitting at the magdalene's vanity and she is painting my
nails where they poke out of the makeshift cast on my arm.
their surface is the deep iridescence of the marbles big and
heavy we used to play with on the little hillock next to our
classroom. i wonder if my brother has reached you yet. i look
at the roman helmet on the vanity

    try it on
    no seriously

she plops the rusting can atop my head and it is much too big for me
and she laughs

    very masc

and she begins to do my eyelashes

    it was his

i watch her face and watch its muscles hold a tense slackness

        he's gone now

she shrugs. people fall out of stories

later she takes me shopping with her at the market and insists i press
my nose to the lavenders and the orange oils and thumbs through
bookstalls and comic racks and laughs kindly and indulgently
whenever i tell her about you

    oh sweetie. your boyfriend sounds really nice and
    i get that you have this whole anxious attachment style thing going
    on but

    i don't believe in miracles
    i've seen too many of them

    seems to me if i were god then
    miracles are just what you do
    to clean up your own fuck-up

i just don't want you to get hurt. plenty of dudes are gods
in my experience it doesn't end great for their fuck buddies
take it from an old gorgon

i feel this settle somewhere into the sediment of me as she buys us a pile of
Archie double digests and a bag of Sour Patch Kids which she says are for
later but which she opens immediately

on the edge of the forest jonathan and david parted and wept

and jonathan said:
     if my father intends to slay you
     i will cast from my bow an arrow over the battlement
     and then you will know to flee

and they kissed one another
and wept upon one another
     but jonathan promised:

       the lord will be between me and you
       and
     between your seed and mine
     forever

and saul bellowed his rage at his pervert prince
     summoning demons from the witch-queen to tell his fortune

     casting all his kingdom into pitch and shadow to revenge himself
     upon david his son's defiler
     the thief of his golden crown

     and from the window of the tower jonathan loosed his secret arrow
                     and david saw where it fell

                     and fled

on the roof of the summer house at magdala she and i watch the sunset
fussily change the colours on the sea like a picky teen choosing a phone
background

her sister martha comes up the stairs and huffs, which i have learned is
her primary way of communicating, and sets down two sandwiches

>women help with housework you know

>no one asked for sandwiches, martha

>um thank you

i manage to peep
but martha does not hear me and glares and complains about the mess
downstairs and uses a name that is not mary. when her sister leaves she
sees me looking for the sting but instead she just says

>god i love when she puts potato chips on the side

the waves lave at the shore a laundry machine chugging through its
cycles as i watch her sister's unkindness rinse against the rock of her,
and she shrugs as she feels my glance

>it is mary
>however contrary

>sometimes you have to listen
>for a name that is different from the one they gave you

>peters and pauls and marys
>god renames those he loves

i look at my nails which she painted
which are very stupid. nothing at all
but made me feel so happy
>and think of my mother who i always remember as crying
>and my father who i always remember as yelling
>and i wonder what i might have found the courage to become if not
for all the scar tissue inhibiting my limbs

lobsters are immortal they say
they die only because they stop being able to moult when the
cicatrices of their exoskeletons adhere
they die tangled in the dead slough they can't shed
lord, we know what we are
but not what we may be

martha appears again at the landing and grumps:

some smelly hippie is here
i will make him a sandwich too i guess

and mary woggles her eyebrows at me as my back stiffens like a terrier

well well well
ecce homo

one day they asked him:
>> the billionaires
>> the glass mega-churches
>>> the anarchists the nuclear family the 2.5 children the grandmas
>> on fixed-income pensions the retiree with pre-existing conditions

should we pay taxes?

and he blanked for a moment, and boggled at the thought
>> as though he was trying for a second to remember what money was
>> and maybe he honestly was, for in all the time i had known him i had
never seen him pay for a sandwich or a haircut or a cup of coffee
>> and the traitor with his chronic halitosis had the management of
our purse

and he was constantly borrowing donkeys rent-free
>>>> sometimes two at a time for some reason
>> really because matthew wanted to fulfill a prophecy (matt loves
>> fulfilling prophecies) but he doesn't really understand classical jewish
>> poetry conventions where you repeat something with elaboration of
>> detail for emphasis:

>> *riding on a donkey,*
>>> *on a colt, the foal of a donkey*

>> like that's one donkey, matt
>> but so sometimes now because of this you see weird renaissance
>> paintings where he's on a donkey, but also using another, second,
>> smaller donkey at the same time as like a weird footstool?
>>> seriously look it up

and actually (sorry i know this is a digression) but even whether he owned
anything at all is debated by the Franciscans
>> because the robe that was ripped from him at the cross-foot and
gambled for, which was seamless (his mom made it for him—so sweet!),
was all he had, if he had anything (Eco is all over this)
>>> and it hangs now whole in Trier
>>>> authenticated by the stigmatist Therese Neumann
>>> and somehow also in pieces in Argenteuil

where they cut it up to keep it safe during the French Revolution
which seems to me a very French way to keep something safe
        and also in a Mtskheta crypt
                authenticated by Nectarius, Archbishop of Vologda
        and for a while one of them even hung in the Winter Palace
        a treasure of the Tsar
anyway there's a movie about it—the robe, not the Tsar
        it's ok swords and sandals stuff, Richard Burton is pretty good
in it at least
        but like kind of misses the point of the whole *behold: they even took his*
robe thing

        sorry—back to the hobo giving financial advice

        should we pay taxes?

and he said does anyone here have a coin?
        (because he didn't)
and someone did, and gave it to him
and he said so this is your coin?
and the dude said yes, obviously
and he said whose face is this, on your coin?
and the guy said the emperor's (which is a graven image, btw)

and he said oh, i see
           well

        render unto Caesar what is Caesar's
                and unto God what is God's

             and give everyone exactly what they deserve

and i don't really think that was an answer, to be honest
           and i don't remember what happened to the coin

a man threw a banquet and hoped all his friends would come

    but the first had time-sensitive investments to make
    and the second had errands to do that could not wait
    and the third was in love
        and all of them were too busy

    so he filled his house with the poor, the sick, the blind and infirm
        and whoever else was handy

    and told his friends to fuck off

if you are poor now
    you will inherit

if you are hungry now
    you will be fed

if you weep now
    you will laugh

· if you are hated now
    you will be adored

           but if you are wealthy now
              you will be impoverished

           and if you are well-fed
                prepare to starve

        if you've been laughing
           we will hear you weep

       and if you have been adored
              so too were many
    whom the world now knows to despise

the first shall be last
      and the last shall be first

and all the world turned upside down
    and shaken

when i was really little there was a tv show—*The
Waterville Gang*. it was a cheap local thing and i think
it was old, in reruns, long gone even at the time i was
watching it. they were all puppets—fish and whatever.
marine life. i think there was an old lady who was a
clam? or i guess not a clam she was an oyster, because
she had a pearl. little reading glasses and a big pearl
wedged into her spineless cloth mass. and a shark and
a starfish and a turtle

anyway

there was a dolphin. Dodger Dolphin. and i think—i mean this is
stupid, but i had a crush on him? i guess i don't know what that
means, or what that meant, for a kid to be in love with a felt dolphin.
but he had a soft brown body and a kind voice, deep and gentle

then one day there was an episode where something bad happened.
a cave-in, i think? i don't remember right. but dodger was crushed

and when he came out he was different—a different
puppet, the same voice. i think the show must have
just wanted to replace the old puppet—maybe it was
worn out or they just wanted to change the design—
the old one was more of that pointier common
dolphin and the new one was a proper bottlenose,
with that bigger beluga-like head and more animated,
softer eyes. objectively a better design

i remember when he came out of the cave he assured
his friends he only looked different but he was the
same, really

and i remember i cried and cried, and didn't know why

when i google it the new puppet is in a museum, photographed on
their webpage next to a colour swatch so you can see how well the
reddish brown of his velveteen has held up

they don't mention the old one at all

you teach about God

mouthing the words of prophets you would have killed

swearing upon gold and gilt
            spinning clever casuistries and prosperity gospels and
            chick tracts
            and scrub, and scrub
            at sins that would all the seas incarnadine

i hear you reverberate like an empty gong
i hear you squeal from megaphones and geometric glass pulpits

you are devils quoting scripture to your purpose
you are hearts without love

tombs of whitewash, gleaming in the sun
                full of dead men's bones

in the late morning curled with him in the stern of the boat as we bobbed in the scrunching sand of littoral waves: half-folded knuckles wedged against my forehead, warm breath in a patch behind my ear, friendly morning wood poking without insistence in the small of my back

i risked a crack of eyelid and it was over: bright white washing into my optic nerve like a tide pool, scattering whatever swam there in a dart from the crash of light and cooking smells and tuneless whistling

with a grumble at the indignity of being recollected into a person, i pulled what was me from what was him, unspooling myself from his canvas curl with two gentle frigs of his tackle. i hopped from the ship into the wet sand grit, and stooped to wash my hands and face, rubbing a streak of drowsy dry drool that was a mingling of both his and mine from my cheek in the cold surf

even through old deck-baked soles, i felt the difference of the rocks under my feet jagged and sharp—not the soft sandy delta of civil little capernaum, but downstream and across the overnight sea, this was the coast of the decapolis: gadara, hippus, gerasa—the greek colonial frontier, upon which strange gods and rome's haunches squatted low, a province untumbled and uncircumcised

behind me on the boat, he pulled himself with a toddler's moan up by the rigging and winked at me, bed-headed, as he thumbed the crust from his eyes. careless of the battered sail behind him, where i noticed several tears rent by the storm that would need to be mended before we sailed again

onshore peter amid chirps scrapes and sea shanties was already frying some sardines above a makeshift fire and under the steep beetling beach cliffs. my brother, always the hiker, had already found his way up the rocky scramble from behind, and waved to us from atop the verge, windmilling his arms to signal we should join him, which none of us were in any rush to do

we still had fish in our teeth when we heard a yelp from the cliff above us. on the rippling shadow cast on the water we could see:

someone else was standing next to james

when they hate you, remember:
        they also hated me

if you were of their world
then they would love you

        you are not
        you never will be

and the day will come when they will murder you
    in streets
    in clubs
    in homes

and say they do it
for the love of god

but they have known
    neither my father
    nor me
    nor the love that binds us
        him to me
        and
        me to you

remember me
when the world does not
    as i will remember you

love one another
when the world does not
    as i have loved you

peter and i scrambled round the backside of the cliff and up its broken spine, through the bright white shattered slabs of a paupers' graveyard, littered with pig-shit and crack-faced statues:

> the imbecile gods of hog farmers and peasants, who perhaps glittered with imperial majesty on the acropolis and on the flower-strewn biers of palatine triumphs, but here managed only downmarket, knockoff grins: jabbering, walleyed, copyright-broken

the stench too was unbearable. as we broke from the rim of the churchyard i saw why: in a muddy, befouled basin overlooking the sea, a field of bristling hogs rutted and grunted, squealing with anxiety that ricocheted full of frets from my brother and the figure that crouched atop him, filthy hands upon his robes, nails seeking purchase in his meat

> *once around the grass*
> *and twice around the lass*
> *and thrice around the maple tree*

the man was naked and caked in scabs, sides lacerated in streaks like a fish's gills and in crisscross against his wrists—self-inflicted or the agitation of breaking free of bindings i could not tell. screaming, trying to drag and muscle james over the cliff and dash him on the stony beach. until

> *who is the third who walks beside you*
> > *who is the fourth who stands in the furnace*

when he saw you the man's entire manner changed: back straightened, limbs unkinked, as though some huge hand had tugged upon the string of a twisted necklace, a puppet pulled from slack, a dismissed courtier remembering a solemnity he had not thought to honour

and the man who was as a bag of broken glass spoke
> with a voice of razorblades
> as a radio cycling through its channels

what hast thou to do with me
son of the most high?   *red sky of morning o ghastly glories of saints*
                       i hear them
                       with hollow shriek the steep of delphos leaving

i count dead limbs of gibbeted gods
solitude filth ugliness
            ashcans and unobtainable dollars children screaming under the
      stairways boys sobbing in armies
            a two-handed engine at the door
                  smites but once, and smites no more

thou shalt conquer o pale galilean
                  the world shall grow grey from thy breath
      we shall drink of the dregs Lethean
                  and feed on the fullness of death

and you cried enough!
and the voice that was many voices fell silent

now the marvel is this: we are consecrated and dedicated to God
that we may thereafter think, speak, meditate, and do nothing
except to His glory. for a sacred thing may not be applied to profane
uses without injuring Him whom we serve

if we, then, are not our own but His, it is clear what error we must flee, and
whither we must direct all the acts of our life

> we are not our own
> let not then our way be swayed by our meagre reason nor our
> wilfulness

> we are not our own
> let us therefore not seek what is easy for us according to the flesh

> we are not our own
> let us forget ourselves and all that is ours

conversely:

> we are His
> let us therefore live for Him and die for Him

> we are His
> let His wisdom and will therefore rule all our ways and deeds

> we are His
> let all the parts of our life accordingly strive ever toward Him

> He who is our only lawful end

> —calvin

and you said who are you?

and the reply came from the ataxic figure and the cries of hogs and the
stones with broken faces and a rolling thunderbent sea

daughters of the lilin
labourers bound in a ring to serve
       for a time and times and half a time
       engineers of the world screech-owls and ostriches dwelling in its ruins
       we who made the flesh of man and would dwell in it
          a world topful of direst cruelty
       pumped till stretchmarks seam across its bloated coast with our seed and
malice
       we are legion for we are many
          spilt like spelt across the surface of this world
              into its every crack and fissure
          and rising in empire

    please, do not hurt us
              send us not back into the darkness
       into the thick black ink
          below the waters on which thou sat'st brooding
             ash and cinders of failed universes

       leave us the light to soothe the scars
          blistered and raised by thy father's lightning

          let us breathe awhile yet the wafting balm of
             the soft, delicious air

    send us into the pigs
            be a god of mercy at least once to us
       disinherited
              your firstborn sons
and till checkout time and trumpet blast
we will trouble you no more

and you grimaced, and it was done

                              and the hogs began to scream
and we watched as the prickling field of flesh cast themselves from the
                       cliffs and drowned the coast by scores

        dashed to gory shreds and fat rinsing in the reddening sea

once there was a wealthy man. and in bed he
said to himself:

tomorrow i shall invest widely and carefully,
diversify my stock portfolio, and plant and sow
with diligence

so shall my storehouses be filled, and my mind
and heart at peace

and that night he died

i pulled off my shirt to put over the man of scabs and filth as he fell shrieking crumpled to the ground sullying himself and seizing and then wept like a child, a dam burst all at once. you crouched and put your hand to his matted thinning crown

>it's ok
>know yourself again

and we carried him down past the broken gods and washed him in a crooked little stream that found its way in a humble, embarrassed dribble to the sea

together you sat as the man dried and warmed by our fire, swaddled in some wrapping from aboard, and as the water by degrees lapped itself clean of its befoulment like a huge cat curled tonguing itself after its predations. i worked on mending the sail, trying not to mind the chill as the sun departed and the sea breeze purpled the sky and hardened my nipples to pebbles, and watched you talk softly, peter and james returning from town with food and loud laughter, and saw something almost like dignity creep into the muffled shape

as night fell the king of kings climbed in next to me on the ship and pushed your thumb gently against my ass-crack and smiled tiredly, the rigging of your face slackened by the day. onshore the man stood, still wrapped in the ship's blanket, stood straight and still

>let me come with you

on board the rigging of your face crinkled again, the pulleys folding your forehead. and you shook your head

i watched your gaze hit the cliffs, still spattered with blood, where the whole town's economy had hurtled into the churn. this place that had left a man to suffer on its edges and now would wake to find itself confounded

>that would be the easy thing
>i never ask that

the chains they made for you are off
show yourself to the ones who put you in them

let them see what they bought
and how much it was worth the paying

teach them: that to be whole we must ruin everything
when you're done
we're just across the sea

and we sailed into a night that
had in its innocence quite forgot the day

at the fountain of bethesda where the five porticoes stand
the archangel raphael
      beautiful and perfect
      and cruel
would descend by turns and trouble the waters

and upon they who were first to touch
its hyaline surface
as the fountain burbled with grace
      scrambling to show their ardency and faith
      then
would he rotate the grand clockwork of the universe
      grinding its mechanisms like a gumball machine
and
      dispense a miracle
to make their bodies whole

but before the mighty angel
      who had once seen satan flung
      from the crystal battlements and hurtle
      headlong in his nine days fall
could bestow his munificent daily blessing
at the rear of the muddled throng he saw:

    you
in your dirty too-small t-shirt
      printed with a logo from a marathon that
    you did not run

      [some reap and others sow
      you said to me at the thrift store when you
      tried it on]

and
the angel frowned, perplexed as you
    waved cheerfully up at him
    invisible, six-wing hovering
greeting him from where you squatted under
one of the arches near a man
twisted on his smelly mat
                who whined that no one helped him
                who ought (the angel thought)
                justly to have shown the face of
                god that he could help himself

and as the principality and power's toe
touched down and rippled the fountain waters
                and the crowd surged desperate to snatch
                their black friday blessing
the angel saw to his exasperation that at the back you had
already rendered the beggar untwisted
                with a perfunctory blessing
                and who now heaved his lousy mat
                onto his bony shoulders
                and thankless left the porches behind

unfairly got
unjustly bestowed
unearned unargued unobeyed

and the man in his unworthiness and cowardice
immediately betrayed you to the authorities
for healing
                indeed when you should not have
                on a holy day
                in a holy place

but you had not given your name
and had vanished in the crowd

and as the mass swarmed the water
the many you had left unblessed
            for the angel to care for

            [till the romans came and sacked the city
            and deconsecrated the fountain
            and gave it to asclepius
            chasing the angel like a pigeon from the rafters

            till a sculptress rebuilt the font in central park
            and turned raphael into a sturdy lesbian
            for angels can both sexes perform, or neither]

and as you scrambled away
the archangel raphael remembered
      long ago:
                  a young man on a dock
                  who had smiled at him, and touched his arm
                        as they reeled in a wriggling fish
                        onto the sticking sand

                  a boy whom the angel had loved
                        as he had loved nothing

                  whom the angel had given away
                        to a princess
                        to be her handsome husband
                        as god had foreordained

and the angel, all unfallen
did not weep

you cannot plant thorn trees
and harvest grapes
and figs are not plucked
from the thistles

and they came to him and asked:
>
> if heaven's so real then
>
> what happens if a woman marries seven times
>
> like if her husbands keep dying
>
> so she had seven husbands
>
> whose wife will she be in heaven?

and he said:

> please do not ask me stupid fucking questions

a sonnet to the asshole
translated from the french
[octet by verlaine; sestet by rimbaud]

mauve rosebud, a puckering gentle pink
an earthy twitch set in a humid loam
gasps small and shy amid the love-spent foam
as skimming cream runs down a frothing sink

filament ooze tossed up a churning shore
seeps down proud hills, and over bruising sides
to your raw, red knot that blooms—abused, untied
that sucks, and seethes, and sighs, and slackens sore

in dreams i kiss this tawny olive musk
in thoughts i sip spent juice from out its husk
the taste of me mixed there with taste of you

the sup of god, the distillation sweet
your living font i ache to drink, to eat
and taste the promised land in thickening dew

before you build a tower
　　　you count the cost
　　　you count the bricks

　　　lest you begin
　　　and cannot finish

　　　and the ruin stands to mock you

before you make war
　　　you count your troops
　　　you number your enemies

　　　lest you fail
　　　and must sue for peace

and so understand:

　　　you must forsake everything
　　　lose everything
　　　give everything

　　　before you follow me

a young man came to him and said

> please—help settle the dispute between me and my brothers over my father's will

> and he said: no

give money
        don't lend it

it rained last night
though i did not hear it
    this isle is full of noises
    and when i wake i cry to dream again

        as the world's lungs burst like wineskins, i feel myself
        shrink and harden like a fist at another season of these
        desolations

    when it all began to end, after your mother that was my mother
    was gone
    and stephen lay in pieces

    wandering—up and down, to and fro—the grey sink rim of the
    waterfront
    trying to remember the world before the shroud fell
    before the seven veils all tore

    black, angular, and ugly, riding low in the bobbing water before
hook-stitching under and surfacing a few minutes and masts away—
    a puzzled, furious punctuation mark of a thing, perplexed and
    perplexing

    setting itself while it worked at a careful but busied distance from
    the rough affability of the mallards and screeching anxiety of the
    gulls and

    then on the wood of the dock, in perfect stillness fanning its wings
    outstretched in the early sun

    pinioned

the cormorant is a waterbird that nature, in its cruelty, has not made waterproof. ducks, with their cheerful greasiness, perch like placid cake decorations on the waves, but the cormorant looks always half-sunk, in crisis, always absurdly seeming on the edge of drowning. this is why they must sun themselves; their soggy feathers otherwise keep them perpetually cold and wet—the evolutionary tradeoff they receive to plunge so low and so deep in pursuit of their wriggling twilight prey

for many the poor ill-favoured bird is an icon of the demonic: its otherwise ungainly animal's sunning pose—limbs outstretched, head drooping in solemn silence—is a vicious parody of the crucifixion:

> Thence up he flew, and on the Tree of Life,
> The middle Tree and highest there that grew,
> Sat like a Cormorant; yet not true Life
> Thereby regaind, but sat devising Death
> To them who liv'd; nor on the vertue thought
> Of that life-giving Plant, but only us'd
> For prospect, what well us'd had bin the pledge
> Of immortality. So little knows
> Any, but God alone, to value right
> The good before him, but perverts best things
> To worst abuse, or to their meanest use

it is to many farmers a pest because its ferocious deforesting of branches as it roosts and its corrosively acidic droppings kill whatever tree it squats in. in nesting in the Tree of Life, then, the cormorant foretells its destruction— turning the immortally blossoming tree into the dead wood that would become the planks of the cross

in the water of the harbour is the mismade cormorant. unlovable, inedible, no song but a guttered grumble. wet and cold

waiting for the sun

the fox has a den
and
the bird has a nest

only humans go homeless

you would not recognize me now. my beard is grizzled with coarse
white hair amid the black. the lithe boy you tackled and fucked
silly in a field has thickened and slowed. my right ear has failed.
with it went my ability, however meagre, to sing. never a great voice,
but it was a little joy—a bellowing to bad musicals and worse pop
songs to annoy neighbours and make you laugh. now there is just a
waterbird croak

> without human touch or voice, i feel parts of my self slough off
> and fall away. my skin buzzes; tears came from a dull, flat depth,
> and then one day altogether stop; my face is nailed on and my
> actions distant, as though all of who i was is suspended in some
> foul aspic of bone and fat. i am aerosol, a fibre-optic show-pig, and
> the flesh of my body now feels like a piece of outdated hardware,
> drawered in a tangle of wires, its battery corroding

i remember you holding me at karaoke, the close tight room dripping with
the mingled steam of us, your back tacky with sweat where my hand gathered
fabric there, bellowing into the cheap, dented microphone between us,
cracking at the notes onscreen above the bad melodrama and crispy bangs of
the stock footage, your lungs young and powerful and wet with utmost life

> [whatever you now find weird, ugly, uncomfortable and nasty
> about a new medium will surely become its signature. CD
> distortion, the jitteriness of digital video, the crap sound of
> 8-bit—all of these will be cherished and emulated as soon as
> they can be avoided. It's the sound of failure: so much modern
> art is the sound of things going out of control, of a medium
> pushing to its limits and breaking apart. The distorted guitar
> sound is the sound of something too loud for the medium
> supposed to carry it. The blues singer with the cracked voice is
> the sound of an emotional cry too powerful for the throat
> that releases it. The excitement of grainy film, of bleached-
> out black and white, is the excitement of witnessing events
> too momentous for the medium assigned to record them]

i am the medium that records you now
i am the only instrument that remembers with fidelity your sound

but i feel the tape is breaking
and in the canisters behind the screen the image magentas and sours

would you still find me charming
would your back still slicken with sweat for me
as you held me
as you sang

before you try
to kill the king
make sure your sword is sharp

                    the traitor dangling
             spilt his guts upon the field

my brother
        whose head they lopped off in jerusalem

                  the twin who doubted
                  in india
                  his flesh roasted
the greek
who had followed the baptizer
        crucified in turkey

                                        the patron of lost causes
                                                      in persia
                                                      beneath the axe

                    along with the zealot
                    hacked to pieces

            the kind tax collector
            assassinated at supper

                                                  the first-called
                                    on a saltire
                                    in achaea

                  the short fellow
                  dragged from the temple
                  stoned to death

the wealthy golanite
        in armenia
        skinned alive

                              the rock of faith
                              in rome
                              crucified upside down

            the spare (who replaced the traitor)
            in ethiopia

and the bald pretender
begging from his captors a swift sword death
the coward privilege of a roman
spouting bland milk from the stump

and i alone escaped to tell the tale

change your heart
for the kingdom comes

i wake up to the sound of you cycling through football matches with the
springs of the foldout in my side in the basement of your mother's house
and rub the sleep out of my eyes and spin into you bleary

the cheap sheet twisted up our legs and through our thighs towelling up
the spatters of saccharine stiffening spilled
>   all pure honey crystallizes

>   the smell of you is strong and pungent on my fingers and stubble-
>   burned face and
>   the head of my dick sore and swollen from your artless fumbling
>   teenage grip
>   i reach between your legs half-wanking you in soft tugs and peer
>   through
>   your big feet in the way of the screen with my ear to your chest

your big athlete brother grunts a good morning and pads across the cold
basement tile behind us to the downstairs shower and i scramble to hide
myself but you do not even flinch

and the shower down the hall sputters through old pipes and hisses and
steams as you look at me
>   and press a kiss onto my eyebrow
>   gentle as a labrador collecting acorns

and my soul cracks and runs golden like a soft diner egg over hash browns
while you half-sleep sour rumpled against me

and i stoop my head to take your nipple into my mouth
>   big as toonies you once lamented, soft and dark

>   and feel its tip roll and harden like a cooking mushroom firming
>   and nip, just a little, on the nub
>   and you swat your paw into my hair
>   and cup me to you by the shoulder
>   as though you were absently nursing me

and onscreen beautiful men in lycra slam into each other and upstairs
your mom clatters through cupboards to make breakfast

and saul in his madness wasted all his power and his years pursuing david and
his faction through the wilderness
> and jonathan watched, and warned, and met david in secret
> stealing through his father's house, under cover of night
> night more loving than the rising sun

>> and in the breeze from off the battlements
>> with their beloved's hair upon their chest
>> they each forgot which of them was which

but in the watchtowers and the woods they sought for david
and so saul in his profligacy was depleted when the philistines returned
> their numbers swollen
> their plate renewed
to revenge the giant of gath
and the armies of israel broke beneath their shields

and so david is not there on the heights of mount gilboa when jonathan is killed
> david mighty warrior
> who might have saved the day

>> neither could he prevent the desecrations the philistines visited upon
>> the prince's remains:

>> snapping the belt once hung on David's hips
>> unstringing the bow once held in David's hand
>> breaking the sword once swung from David's thigh
>> denting the plate once laid on David's back
>> tearing the robe once caressing David's belly
>> staining the linens that once brushed David's loins

>> mutilated and ravaged
>> hung from the city walls
>> the butchered beautiful boy that David had so long wept upon

you have heard it said
      do not break your oaths

      but i say to you:
      make no oath at all

      swear no oath to heaven
            for it is god's throne
            beyond your ken

      swear no oath to the earth
            for it is god's footstool
            to use at his leisure
            or dash apart in his rage

      swear no oath to your nation
            for you do not rule it
            and kings are fickle
            and their wills perverse

      swear no oath to your body
            for it will work or fail
            no matter your will

say yes
      or
say no

      believe what you believe
      choose what you choose
      speak what you will and
      do what you can

      love always

the rest is not yours
      to control
      to wield
      to answer for

      and i would not see you latched to evil

for a while at the end she began every new blanket or scarf or hat with some worry that she would never finish it

and then one day she looked up at me from her crochet and gestured at the bales of yarn piled nearby and said in the thick slow slur that had become her voice

    i think i had more eye than tummy

that night i helped take off the cheap shoes she wore and unrolled the stockings from her feet and helped her into her chairlift. and at the top i pressed my hand into her back to steady her as her fingers trembling found the walker with the rosary tangled around its rubber handle. and she kissed my neck, and i her forehead, and she said

    good night. i love you
    meu amor

in the assumptions of art even at the end she is young and whole and spirals upward in a graceful aerial pirouette uncertainly but beatifically from her dormition towards a vertiginous baroque light

because she was perfect and kind and my mom and death cannot touch perfection

it is pretty to think so

the day will come when many will say:

      lord
      i prophesied and preached in your name!

      many devils
      have i tormented, and

      much wickedness
      have i cast out

      where is my reward

and i will say:

    who are you?

    i never knew you as anything
    except an operative of cruelty

      your life served your own malice
      and not me at all

After you were dead and back and gone again, I became gauzed and blurred, a TV tuned to a dead channel.

Then, one day, there was Stephen.

When he spoke it was with the accents of the Decapolis—a dialect rinsed in scores of captivities and exiles and apostasies. When he washed I saw his cut amid the heavy black patch of his fur was low, half-uncircumcised, his parents marking his body to hedge a bet that his spirit fiercely refused.

He had seen your last days in Jerusalem, and caught fire, and in him I saw how your words might be an engine—a way past Rome and past the creeping hibernation that thrummed my skin.

When he looked at me I know he saw something broken, and he spoke like a man to a bird with a twisted wing.

As we gave out sandwiches and soda cans in the Temple, he tricked me into laughing, and his curly hair when he bent down to reach into the cooler under the table smelled like peppercorn. When he touched my hand it was so soft I shivered.

And the crowd swelled to get food, and to listen to this beautiful man wrap your name in his lilt.

He was quicksilver and he was strong and he was kind.

And he wasn't you.

and in the hand of the enthroned i saw a book
    sealed with seven seals

    and i wept, for none was fit to open it

    but behold arise:

        lion of judah
                    root of david

            lamb who was slain
            for every kin and tongue and nation

    and he took the book
    and read

after his death at the hands of the philistine horde the pieces of jonathan's
flesh are recovered, and burnt, and buried beneath a tree with the ashes of
his father saul

    who himself died ignobly
        whether by suicide or a servant's hand
        the text and history are unclear
        but david has the servant who claims to have done it killed
    regardless

when david hears the news from gilboa
his grief is terrible

        and the boy david
        who was born a shepherd
        is made king
        and judah and israel are made one crown

and the poet-king sings an elegy for the lost prince jonathan. and david
decrees forever after that the children of the united kingdom of israel be
taught the lament of the bow, his song for jonathan

    lost on gilboa's heights
    whom the king loved as himself

the lament of the bow
song of david for jonathan

o israel
your glory lies slain on your heights
and how fallen are the mighty

tell it not in gath:
        proclaim it not in the streets of ashkelon
        lest the daughters of the philistines rejoice
        lest the uncircumcised exult

oh mountains of gilboa
        neither dew nor rain befall you
        no showers touch your terraced fields
        may you dry and crack
        may your meadows shrivel your grain

        for there his mighty shield is shattered
        no longer anointed in oil

from the blood of the slain
from the fat of the mighty
        the bow of jonathan never fled
        the sword of saul supped hungrily

swifter than eagles, stronger than lions
saul and jonathan, beloved and delightful in life
        were not divided in death

o daughters of israel
weep for saul
        who clothed you in scarlet and pomp
        who decked you in ornaments of gold

how the mighty are now fallen
dear jonathan slain on your heights

i will weep for jonathan
     who was my sole delight
     your love to me was all i had extraordinary
     surpassing the love of women

how the mighty have fallen
and all the tools of war are broken

and i saw the lamb begin to open the seals of his book
    and i heard a noise as of thunder

and one of the four beasts saying, come and see
    and i saw:

    and he opened forth the seals of his scroll

    and the first seal:
        a white horse
            in his rider's hand a bow
            and forth he went to afflict

    and the second seal:
        a red horse
            in his rider's hand a sword
            and forth he went to slaughter

    and the third seal:
        a black horse
            in his rider's hand the scales
            and forth he went to famish

    and the fourth seal:
        a pale horse
            who was Death
            and after followed Hell

and forth they furled across the world:

    with pest, with sword, with hunger
    and the power of the grave

one day they pulled stephen from our stall and dragged him outside the city and stripped him and hurled stones at him the size of apples for his blasphemies

his eye was on me and not on me and was full of forgiveness and kindness
          when it popped and sludged like a grape

and as the rocks raised welts and broke apart joints he cried out:

          I see the Heavens open
                    and the Son of Man standing at the right hand of God!

and his face was like the face of an angel as the rocks smashed it apart into gore and bone

          this is how you treat your friends

and i saw the lamb open the fifth seal

    and from beneath the altar
        churning from the sluices of its offal
        seeping from its gutters

i heard the voices of the unjust slain
burst forth to demand:

    how long o lord
    shall we stay for your justice

        how long o lord
        shall we be unavenged

watching the sinews of Stephen's body tenderize and unzip
was Saul, a bald cruel man with a keen high voice, breathing
threats and murder

Saul

> who fell down drunk at Damascus
> and dared to say he saw your ineffable face

Saul

> who would number himself among us
> and elbow his way to your table

Saul

> who sold our birthright to Rome
> and who you would make your instrument

Saul

> who laughed to see the heretic boy struck to pieces
> under the capital's high white walls

i remember once we came upon a town where a local sorcerer was doing
ramshackle exorcisms, using your name like a magic spell
     and my brother in his temper almost shook the bonestrewn hut to
pieces
     like a mob enforcer guarding your turf

        do not prevent him or
        any good done in my name

beholding saul and his mighty deeds i see
you ought to have been more careful of your infringed copyright

i do not know what to do with these strangers who flout your banner
how to hold them to account
how to wear the vestments they soil in mud and blood

you gave your name to every mountebank and now they run it
through the gutters and in your profligacy i have nowhere to spend
its coin

this weekend they found more mass graves
hundreds of students from the residential schools
buried hugger-mugger by the nuns and priests

at the knife-edge of monstrosity come men in robes always to call it saintly
before the end all holy things are profaned

      you would not let us throttle the hucksters who used your name
            because we had to account for them
            they are ours to answer for

and on thursday as an elderly bride and groom posed with grandchildren for
photos for their sixtieth wedding anniversary outside the cathedral, a woman
came to the church's door and splashed it with her bucket of red paint

and carefully, deliberately pressed her hand over and over again in the paint
and upon the grain of its wood

      until her hands had made many hands that seeped and ran and
      pooled on the steps and towards the assembled generations below

      and she wrote: WE WERE CHILDREN

and i wonder:

were you inside your father's house
the lights off
with your ear pressed to the vandalized door
as her palm fell over and over

              or in the crowd
              watching with horror
              at the scandal of atrocities done in your name

were you mixed in the bucket, as sacrament turned paint to blood

              or were you as ever
              in the grave

and returned from death he flamed
fire and life incarnate
                                    back and gone forever
                                    my darling clementine

you see me now as i am

therefore i have suffered none of the things which they will say of me
                        i wish it to be called a mystery

for what you are, you see that i showed you
            but what i am, that i alone know, and no one else

as for seeing me as i am, i have told you this is impossible
            until you are as i am

        you hear that i suffered
                        yet i suffered not

        that i suffered not
                        yet i did suffer

        that i was pierced
                        yet i was not wounded

        that i was hanged
                        yet i was not hanged

        blood flowed from me
                        yet it did not flow

        those things that they say of me
                        i did not endure
                                        and the things that they do not say
                        those i suffered worst of all

and he came to the riverbank of jordan
and he said:

baptize me
make me your disciple
and i shall write you in my book
but if you do not
then erase me from your scroll

but the baptist replied:

you have lied to the people
deceived the common and the priest
in your sodomies and wickedness cut off the seed of men
that is due to the wombs of women
you have loosed the sabbath till it broke
cheated the multitude with the music of the horn
and played false melodies with the trumpet

no i will not baptize you, for
> the deaf cannot become a scribe
> the blind cannot write a letter
> a house in ruins cannot prosper
> a widow cannot become a bride
> putrid waters cannot purify
> and a stone cannot flow with oil

but he replied:

ah, but
> the deaf *will* become a scribe
> the blind *will* write a letter
> the ruined house *will* prosper
> the widow *will* become a bride
> putrid waters *will* purify
> and a stone *will* flow with oil

and the baptist said:

if you can explain this
then you are a wise messiah

    and he said:
    the deaf shall turn scribe when the unborn child is grown
    the blind shall write clearly when the wicked man reforms
    the ruin shall prosper when the wealthy ruler is humbled
    the widow shall wed when her heart is mended
    filthy water shall purify when it has flowed through all the earth like a
    whore
    and a stone shall flow with oil when from the dry and faithless heart
    kindness pours on orphan, old, and widow

and the spirit told the baptist to take the man to the jordan and baptize him
and the spirit fell upon him as a dove

    and Life is Praised, and Life triumphs!

            —The Book of the Baptist

and he sat at a well
in samaria
a region we ought not to have been in
at the foot of a mountain
that was holy, but not to us

and he asked a woman of the region
    can you give me a drink?

and she said:
    where's your bucket?
    for the well is deep and
    you know your people and i can't share

and he sighed
    listen
    if you knew who asked you for a drink
    you'd ask *me* for a drink of living water
    so that you'd never be thirsty again

and she said:
    hmm
    seems like you still don't have a bucket though

    but if you can make it so i never get thirsty again
    you can have the fucking bucket

and he said:
    where's your man?

and she said:
    i haven't got a man

and he said:
    haha ok well true enough
    because you've had *five*
    and the current guy's not even yours

and she said:
    who are you?

and he said:
      oh
      i'm the messiah
      haven't actually told anyone that yet

      well too late
      so i'll tell you this too:

      someday our temple in the south will be gone
      smashed to pieces by rome
      and someday this mountain will be deserted
      but the god we both love
      and who loves us both
      will be standing still

and she went into town
telling everyone of the man she had met
and at the well she left behind her bucket

the followers of the baptist are still with us
a small cluster of them
the mandaeans
mostly in san antonio texas
about 2,500 people still dunking in the guadalupe river
to the confusion of the local rotary board

and the samaritans still worship at mount gerizim
with a different ten commandments
only 870 of them left now

the world is littered with these endangered species of faith
like pockets of holy pandas
turning small sombre somersaults
        flocks we know not of
        of a different fold

and the woman at the well
whose name, they say, was photina
luminous one, who took the first snapshot of you
went home to her family
and the man who was not her husband
and became the first apostle
founding a variant mutant faith
whose taxonomy and creed we have forgotten
when history remembers her at all
and bothers to make up her name

and so the woman who you promised would never be thirsty
spread that faith even to rome, even to the imperial palace
and was thrown by furious nero
with his usual flair for irony and camp
into a bone-dry well

at the bottom of everything
in the dark
at the altar of an unknown god that was you all along
she probably must have thought it was
a little funny, at least

when she died

LOVE: Reason, you shall always be
half-blind
you and all who are nourished by
your doctrine

        for to see what is only before your eyes
        yet not to know it
        is to be always peering
        through a glass
        darkly

REASON: and who are you, Love?
are you not also one of us
        a virtue
        though of us the greatest?

LOVE: I AM GOD
for love is god
and god is love

        and the little soul that speaks us
        in her humble cell
        through her love
        is even god herself

thus this precious beloved of mine
        taught by me
        guided by me
        is changed in a twinkling
        outside herself entirely
for she is transformed into me

        —marguerite porete
        translated from the french
        [unrecanted
        for which the author burned]

on the seventh day god rested
and as he slept his subjectivity splintered
skin cracking like cicada husk to powder
subdividing like cells like blistering mitosis
each cell a living god
and the breath on the water cast the seeds
like mustard like figs like twists of sycamore
spiralling

and the god-spore rooted where it landed
across the universe like yeasting dust
in the foundations and the high places
upon the rock amid the bushes
in the deep soil and the shallow
and became life
abundant and abounding

and so god woke to regard themself
male and female created
all sex and neither
peering out of so many eyes
beneath so many secret crowns

and the politic angels fell lamenting
when they saw the empty throne
and cast at its foot their broken diadems
heaped atop sceptres of iron and gold
long laid by
for of regal sceptre there was no need
and god was all in all

i held stephen's leftover body for a long cold time, until the tender soiled
rags of him were cool and the blood on my arms was sticky and stank

      burst bowels like a ladybug purpling a cruel child's nail

i knew then what kind of world they would make of you
and what bright light he saw rising

and i saw in bright radioscopic clarity what was to come

      i left the last of my tears in the nape of his neck

          for the world that might have been
          if you had been a little more guileful and guileless

      for the boy i had been
      who had wiped your seed from himself on a beach in galilee
      and dreamt that beach and i might have been enough

      for him and for you
      and for what little was left of me

and the next day i walked away
and from my sandals i shook the dust

the magdalene's complaint

Sith my life from life is parted,
>   Death come take thy portion;
> Who survives when life is murdred,
>   Lives by mere extortion:
> All that live, and not in God,
> Couche their life in deathe's abode.

Selye starres must nedes leve shyninge
>   When the sunne is shadowed,
> Borowed streames refrayne their runninge
>   When hed-springes are hindered:
> One that lives by other's breathe,
> Dyeth also by his deathe.

O trewe life! sith Thou hast left me,
>   Mortall life is tedious;
> Death it is to live without Thee,
>   Death of all most odious:
> Turne againe or take me to Thee,
> Let me dye or live Thou in me!

Where the truth once was and is not,
>   Shadowes are but vanitye;
> Shewinge want, that helpe they cannot,
>   Signes, not salves, of miserye.
> Paynted meate no hunger feedes,
> Dyinge life eche death exceedes.

With my love my life was nestled
>   In the summe of happynes;
> From my love my life is wrested
>   To a world of heavynes:
> O lett love my life remove,
> Sith I live not where I love!

O my soule! what did unloose thee
           From thy sweete captivitye,
    God, not I, did still possesse thee,
           His, not myne, thy libertie:
    O too happy thrall thou wert,
    When thy prison was His hart.

Spitefull speare that brak'st this prison,
           Seate of all felicitye,
    Workinge thus with dooble treason
           Love's and life's deliverye:
    Though my life thou dravst awaye,
    Maugre thee my love shall staye.

                —robert southwell

again we came upon a stranger baptizing in your name. immediately
james was in the water trying to stop him when we heard you laughing

        i am the way
        the truth
        the life

if no man can receive blessing unless given to him from heaven
then all blessings must be from heaven

and none can come to me
unless the Father who sent me draws him

if anyone hears my words and does not believe
i do not judge him
i did not come to judge the world
but to save the world

do you think i do not know my children?

even if they do not know my name
i know theirs
        and i have many names you do not know

        i am all ways
        all truths
        all life

        the good shepherd has many flocks
                many folds
                    whose fleece and fields you will not live to see

and each sheep knows his master's voice when he calls

and on the road from the city philip met qinaqis
      a eunuch sworn in service
      to the mighty queen of ethiopia
      and who was keeper of the royal treasury
      riding in a magnificent chariot
           returning to their home
           many leagues away

and qinaqis had paused in their journey
and was under the shade of a tree
reading aloud
      (which was the manner of the age)
from the scroll of the prophet isaiah
about the suffering and the meekness of the lamb

and philip asked the magnificent figure
with a boldness that surprised himself:
      do you know who this is about
      and what it is that it promises?

and qinaqis was startled
and they said:
      how can i
      unless someone teaches me?
and they invited philip to join them in the chariot
and the two talked as they rode

and they came to a river
and the eunuch who was a foreigner said:
      look. here is water! cold and clean
      what can stop me from being baptized?

and philip said to qinaqis
      who was neither gender and was both
      who was servant of a distant queen:

      nothing can
      the water is for all

and together they went down to the water
      and the peasant philip shed his cambric
      and the courtier qinaqis shed their gold
and qinaqis was baptized

      and when philip was gone
      (transported to azotus)
      qinaqis continued home
      bringing fire

      for great was the learning of qinaqis
      and greater still was their ardour

      and the church of ethiopia
         grew mighty
         and grew wise

      and its library was the envy of all the world
      and its wisdom teaches the nations still

         saint qinaqis
         pray for us

let no stranger say:
  the lord will exclude me from his people

and let no eunuch complain:
  i am but a stricken branch

for rather
this is the word of the lord:

  the eunuch who keeps my covenant

    i will make for them a home
    they will dwell in my own house

    i will build for them a monument and memorial
    better than that of either sons or daughters

    i will give to them an everlasting name
    that will endure forever

  and

  the stranger who keeps my covenant

    i will bring them to my holy mountain
    i will give them joy in my house of prayer

    i will make them glad

    and all their prayers and sacrifices
    i will see blazing upon my altar

for my temple shall be a house of prayer
for all nations
and all peoples

   amen

to know the world
but not yourself

is to know nothing at all

some are born eunuchs
            some become eunuchs
            some live as eunuchs

                    for the glory of the kingdom

[eusebius testifies that origen reading this underwent an orchiectomy
[eusebius may have been mistaken
[eusebius may have been correct
[eusebius admired origen

[origen was foundational to the church
[origen has never been canonized as a saint
[origen's views were deemed denigrating to marriage and reproduction

[origen's self-castration was a scandal   or
[origen's self-castration was malicious gossip   or
[origen's self-castration never happened   or
[origen's self-castration was self-actualization   or
[origen's self-castration was origen's own business

        [theophilus called origen "the hydra of all heresies"
        [justinian ordered that origen's writings should be burned
        [origen's writings persist

[origen has not written in some centuries

[if origen wrote today, new words and conceptual models might have been
available to expand the categories previously delineated by:
                ["born eunuchs"
                ["become eunuchs"
                ["live as eunuchs"

[we do not need origen to do this work
[we do not need the master's speech to do this work
[we do not need any speech to do any work
[the speech, nonetheless, persists

[let those who can accept this accept this

as a drop of water disappears
in a vat of wine
>
> and tastes of wine
>
> and blushes in its colour

as iron in the fire quickens
becomes as the fire
>
> and flashes red
>
> and runs to liquid molten

as the air on a sunny day brightens
and is transformed
>
> and suffuses with sunlit glory
>
> and is sunshine itself

so must the saints
so must all human feeling
>
> melt and dissolve
>
> and flow into God

otherwise how shall God be all in all
if something survives of us?

but perhaps
but doubtless
the substance will remain
though changed
>
> another form
> another glory
> another power
>
> but
> who will this come to?
> who will see it?
> who will possess it?

—bernard of clairvaux

marlowe and james knew what you were
didn't they
wilde knew

       stab socket green carnation uranians
       can always spot half-reluctant trade
       slumming it on docks and in sprezzatura flesh
       ready to unzip if we beg

         you all imagine what you want
         do not try that one on me
         i was there remember
         i remember

the blanket my mom wrapped me in
a faded yellow
her weight is wrong misdistributed now
my arms come from too high up
       your mother was my mother
       man and wife is one flesh
       what then were we?

            derail the magpie mind of me then and check to see if
              there is any scratch draft song to sing. a last tithonic
              shriek before the moon blows down
            and the stars snuff out and the cardinals sound alarm
            at the horrors of the dawn

you left me to dwell in forgeries and
crack!ship apocrypha and a thousand
strangers' sheets. because you cannot edit a
photo in the light that made it

       so be it
       so be it then

       running relay through the seventh circle
       as on my tongue bitter halved zopiclone and
       omnicoastal crocuses bloom

       and in the stale black dark i croak

once at the mall i saw a dead man
a boy, really
    who had fallen from an upper level
    and dashed his brains out upon the concrete near the fountain
    where i had wept for hours once
        when you broke my heart

and i remember a janitor was placing CAUTION cones around the corpse
    slippery when wet
    a mop and bucket at the ready
        unsure if this mess was his
    while the escalator chugged nearby
        and the fountain spouted its trick spit-takes
where the affable angel troubled the water
using healing as a prank

and
    looking down at the red splatter
    while the boy finished leaking
    by where i wept to lose you
    making strange images of death near the ice cream and the ethical
soap store
    a flubbed masterpiece of confusion

i remember being unable to tell:
    was this anguish that had done this?
        or had it been a joke?

had he meant to fall? or tripped?
        or never imagined it would be far enough to hurt him
        or for a moment, childlike, forgotten the stakes:

    a lunatic walking on a flashlight beam
    or a painter in a frenzy
        squeezing out all the tube at once

    accident or sorrow? despair or joy?

how strange:

that they should look
       in the end
         so completely the same

sodom stood tall by the sea
rising above the asphaltic basin
the western sumac all flame
          [it is poison when it grows by water
          they say]

          all around us the green grew dry to ash
          sweating smells of fir and cedar bark
          as crouching cruising in the gloom
          on knees and dirty busy hands
          we slobbered sacred hospitalities to the stranger

and here with sage leaves tangled in his horns and shag
the great god pan upon his mighty haunches

          paused piercing another maenad shepherd boy
          and spied through the brush:
                    a newborn ringed about in star-
          spangled halo mobiles
                    playing with its rattle in a barn trough
          and knew next would come the bulldozers
          to gentrify the ramble
          and comb out all our fur

          seraphic strafing flashlights amid the slime pits
          and at the beach a spotlight boat
          cherub flame behind lucite igniting bitumen
          a tear-gas forest ringed in riot-cop
          who would break our backs to
          straight them

and by the river of acheron
there we sat down and wept

we sit on the concrete stoop of your backyard in the cool of the day
dandelions breaking through the cracking pavement tiles like ugly little
children's prayers bright and selfish

you tried to share your joint with me but i coughed like a big baby and you
rubbed my back hard and smacking and laughed into my hair and then
you said here let me mellow it a little

> what
> it gets softer if someone does it for you
> watch

and you inhaled deep and holding it in your lungs poured smoke into my
mouth like a dragon my eyes wide then closed tight our lips not quite
sealed like vapour incense communion like the cataract of some ancient
quickening waterfall till i was bursting with you

> and in my lungs i hold your breath

and light-headed as you come from my nostrils and lips
and for a moment i sit mingled with you, abuzz
> stupidly good

and after a thousand years staring at the detritus of the yard skids stacked
against a rusting shed i ask hey
> can i ask something

> about your dad

you roll the joint in your big fingers and let ash drop onto the upturned
orisons and don't look at me as you dip between your knees to drag the
stub against the tile and shrug

> my father made things

you begin doodling on the pavement slab with the stump like a black crayon

> very funny

> no really

construction
he was a builder
>
> he supervised subdivisions, did most of sepphoris
>
> > he used to take me to the job site
> > huge dumb guys with big bellies swearing and pissing in
> > bottles page six girls tacked up inside the backhoe

honestly it smelled so beautiful
mud and diesel

> > > nothing smells so good like sawdust

> i helped out in the summer sometimes mowing model home lawns
> and picking up two-by-fours before they laid the sod
> but even when we were little

**you spin to lay your length across the cool of the concrete and put your
holey holy socks on my lap and i can't tell what you want me to do with
them am i supposed to rub them?**

all these hairy dudes in hard hats building perfect little dollhouses
> > like magic
> > like gnomes in a fairy tale

> > .seeing all the houses full of newspapers and zip-lock
> > wrappers and raccoon shit and dicks drawn all over
> > the plywood dark materials building worlds before
> > the families moved in
> dark materials
> redeemed from chaos

> > and then, all of a sudden: finished, a home

**fuck it i start rubbing where the white gym socks have worn the
thickness thin**

> one time i went exploring
> i used to run away a lot

i must have been like six or seven
behind the lots there was this big muddy drybed
all cracked and splitting
        like a red pepper roasting

and dad told me and my sister not to go there and of course
that's exactly where i went right away

right onto the mud
        and i got stuck

my sister started crying and crying and she ran to get my dad
and when i was by myself
sinking in the mud with all the broken bricks the builders
threw out
i thought
                        "this is it"
        in quicksand like the cartoons
        a set of footsteps going to a spot then stopped
        it's weird

        how peaceful it was

you sneer a little, and there's water in your eyes which you swat away
staring at the fence above your head where some dingy city sparrow is,
glances its glance, and then is not

        then my dad swooped over the cliff and saw me and just
                        scooped me up
        like it was nothing
        which of course it was
        just mud
        and brought me back to the dusty truck
                stone dust refined like flour inside
                and turned a garden hose on my boots
                he wasn't even mad

                i guess he understood i had to go
                        had to see what it was like

that feels good

i realize you're finally looking at me and what i'm doing to your feet i'm
humiliated oh i wasn't sure if i

      no it's perfect
      you're perfect
      fuck

you take your big toe and flex it downward to crack it like a knuckle
against the bricks which looks agonizing but you do it all the time and
then you plop it back in my lap and above us in the sky i stare in quiet
admiration at the magnificent ethereal beauty of a star that turns out to
be a plane
which is just humans rocketing through the sky at thirty-five thousand
feet
      nothing special

hey what happened to your parrot

                  what parrot

it is easier to shove a camel through a
needle's eye
than for the rich to enter the kingdom
to come

and so we say that a person must be so poor so abject
        that he is not
        nor leaves any place for god to operate in at all
        for to preserve place is to preserve distinction

and so i pray to god to make me free of god
        for if god is the origin of the creaturely
        then my essential being is above god

for if god's essence is above being and distinction
there too was i and there knew myself to make myself

then i am my own cause according to my essence
        which is eternal
but not according to my becoming
        which is temporal

when i am made hollow
then i am unborn
        and when i am unborn
        then i can never die

then i am what i was
then i neither wax nor wane
then i am an unmoved cause
        that moves all things

        but
        if one cannot understand this sermon
        don't worry about it

                —meister eckhart

the thing is that thomas was kind of an asshole
like not just the wound in the side stuff but pay attention and you
start noticing he always has something shitty to say

this extends beyond the usual canon to include his suspicions
when your mom died
see sometimes she goes to sleep but other times she starts floating
up to heaven like an alien abduction situation
(because she was sinless, and therefore couldn't properly die, which
is the wage of sin, is the idea)
     but tom has his usual doubts
     and so in these cases in several apocryphal versions she
tosses her girdle to him as she's floating up
        to the awed dinner-plate-halo beardos down below
           as a team of cherubic twinks hoists her up the
           halftime show rigging
        like a celebrity tossing a sweaty towel to the crowd
      or a reverse bra thrown at a concert kind of deal
          and thomas catches it

so the little dick can have a souvenir
to believe it really happened

i thirst, thou wounded lamb of god,
to wash me in thy cleansing blood,
to dwell within thy wounds; then pain is
sweet, and life or death is gain.

take my poor heart and let it be
forever closed to all but thee!
seal thou my breast and let me wear
that pledge of love forever there.

how blest are they who still abide
close sheltered in thy bleeding side,
who life and strength from thence derive,
and by thee move, and in thee live.

what are our works but sin and death
'til thou thy quick'ning spirit breathe?
thou giv'st the power thy grace to move;
o wondrous grace! o boundless love!

hence our hearts melt, our eyes o'erflow,
our words are lost; nor will we know,
nor will we think of ought beside
my lord, my love, is crucified.

—nikolaus von zinzendorf
    of the moravians
  translated by the wesleyan workshop

and it is admittedly a little weird theologically
(and not to mention gender-wise)
that seconds after telling the magdalene not to touch you
we smash-cut to thomas knuckle-deep in your new orifice
and weirder still the insistence

        that thomas believed because he saw and touched
        but
        happier are those that believe without seeing

like why should that be
i mean i know why
most people will never see, and it's nice to be nice about it
but is it so bad to want to?

but then maybe it has nothing to do with the mysteries of faith
and everything to do with the gross insistence
on the right
to another's flesh

and the shrill demand to disclose
maybe you just wanted the small dignity
      of being understood

      and of having the people you love
      take you at your word
      without wanting to see the scars

he tenderly placed his right hand on my throat
and drew me towards the wound in his side

     drink, daughter, from my side
      and by that draught your soul shall become enraptured with such
delight that your very body
         which for my sake you have denied
         shall be inundated with its overflowing goodness

    drawn close in this way to the outlet of the fountain of life
i fastened my lips upon that sacred wound
and still more eagerly the mouth of my soul
    and there i slaked my thirst

         —saint catherine of siena

       the mother can lay her child tenderly to her
       breast, but our tender Mother [who is Christ] can
       lead us easily into his blessed breast through his
       sweet open side
       and show us there a part of the godhead and of the
       joys of heaven, with inner certainty of endless bliss

       —julian of norwich

once while visiting tyre in the north a gentile woman who didn't really
know much about your deal asked you to cure her daughter

and you said i must tend to the children before the dogs

     (which was rude)

but she said: well
                even dogs get leftovers

    and so you healed the girl

        because you had to admit
             that was a pretty good comeback

miracles are ugly, inelegant things

   interferences in the game triumphs of ethics over aesthetics
weird hacks that disrupt the glorious concatenation of time and space
unfair, unrepeatable, capricious operations of a mercy whose quality is not
strained

            [in portuguese this is the virtue of *desenrascanço*
                  the art of untangling without skill or grace or training
                  the way a team of chubby uncles can patch a hole in a pipe with
                  duct tape or stack a ladder atop a ladder to fix a busted air
                  conditioner   ]

      fold god into time
collapse the infinite into the crush of cause and effect
      cram the ineffable divine into history
and you end up with some odd behaviour
like a duck tipping under the water, ass in the air, disrupting the ecology
of the tide pool with its big dumb face

      and so for a while god was just a weird little hobo running around
doing his best. addled contents under pressure
      with not much time and only his indiscreet little body to work with
      he leaked grace from every pretty orifice
      using his spit like a grandma to clean the cheek of the world's ills

      like the deaf guy whom he gave a wet willy and shouted *ephphatha!*
      which means "be opened"
      as though he was popping a cork in the guy's head with a magic spell
and elbow grease

      or the blind dude whose eyes he spat in and asked:
                  ok how's that?

      and who replied um i guess it's ok?
            i can sort of see people but
                  they're kind of like trees, walking?
and he said oh shoot
and he tried again adjusting

238

as though he were calibrating lenses at the optometrist
till he got the slobber ratio right

oh that's better

and he said:

honestly i would rather you not mention this to anybody

but the guy did anyway

your saliva has been as a chrism
       bringing hearing to the deaf and causing the blind to see
what then must it have done to me
       hallowed in my whimpering
            holy in my cries
       as you spat to slicken my dilating pucker
       your spittle dribbling down my haunch
       preparing the way of the lord

once there was a woman carrying a jar of meal
       who hadn't noticed a small crack
       and it spilled behind her on the road

       and when she got home, it was empty

when you were gone and the fire descended it seemed pointless to return home. your mother and i stayed in bethany so i could travel to the temple to work with stephen distributing food during the day and help her in the evenings

it was quiet—quiet as i had never known the world could be quiet. there was tea and *Murder, She Wrote* and dishes i left simmering while i worked on the kitchen table and she crocheted in her chair, snug in her soft white cardigan, holding the mesh up to the light to inspect its inerrancy. the air felt mentholated, halfway to hospital we were what was left of you. the indecent cavities at pompeii empty air left where a body had been

one night which felt late but wasn't in that quality of all suburban evenings i asked her the question i had asked you a million times, and to which i had received a million answers:

was it true?

"if i should begin to tell you, fire will issue forth out of my mouth and consume all the world," she warned. and then in a million voices she said:

ELPHUE ZARETHRA CHARBOUM
NEMIOTH MELITHO THRABOUTHA
MEPHNOUNOS   CHEMIATH
AROURA   MARIDON   ELISON
MARMIADON   SEPTION
HESABOUTHA   ENNOUNA
SAKTINOS ATHOOR BELELAM
OPHEOTH ABO CHRASAR

she turned back to her needlework and her eyes twinkled as yours used to: "sorry just a joke." next to the plastic tupperware tray with her pills she was so small. i remembered her holding your broken body, stretched out like a linebacker atop her buckling frame, as though the force of your mass would push through her and pierce like a lance to the nickel core of the earth

then she looked out the window, into a black night, in the space where the garden should be and wasn't

"He was a miracle. I never needed him to be anything else."

and in teacup silence and night like a blanket her needlework and our wounds stitched themselves by inches

the magnificat

> my soul augments the greatness of the lord
> and my spirit delights in him
>> my god
>> my saviour
>
> for he has beheld me
>> his lowly servant
>> and all to come will call me blessed
>
> he has done great deeds
>> for me
>> for those before and those to come
>> and ever holy is his name
>
> he has dashed apart the works of the proud
>> and flung the mighty from their thrones
>> to uplift the lowly and the humble
>
> he has cast the rich starving from their tables
>> and fed the hungry with his feast
>
> he has remembered his promise to our fathers
>> to the children of his people
>> to bring mercy and
>> to bring hope
>
>> forever and ever
>
>>> amen

when i die feed me to birds
    let the red raw fly
    wrap me in mushroom under a tree
    let my boiled clean skull
    play an amateur production yorick
    press the ash to diamonds
    ethical and lab-grown
    then set them in tacky keepsake rings
        and lose them

it was warm
i remember the womb of it
the order the parts of me were shaped the stage on
which i place the mount of the skull
i remember the first flashings
and the shaping of my throat and feeling my legs
articulate the world in fits
i remember the shell we built on i remember the great
mineral crystal symphony the whirling aura the brass

i remember a feeling of feeling my way to being
the twitch of my heart and sphincter but that came
later it was a kind of surging first

like the feeling of being wet grain moving or something
like the thrum epithalamion not the thing but the
feeling the taste of epithalamion

the flutter of my phalanges the ticking the piano i
understood but not now understand
        when the moving the hole the sharp

i am stuck in the motor of the way to you
i will burn the web down and find you in the web of it

and i saw a wonder in heaven:

      a woman clothed with the sun
      the moon under her feet
            and upon her head a crown of twelve stars

      and she was with child
            and pained to be delivered

and i beheld a great red dragon
      with seven crowned heads and ten horns
      who in its tail drew a third of heaven

      who stood before the woman
            to devour her child

and the woman sun-clothed brought forth a son
      to rule all the nations with a rod of iron
      and he was caught up to the throne
            and the woman fled to the wilderness

and there was war in heaven
      michael and his angels against the dragon

        and the dragon
            that old serpent
was cast into the earth

        and here it doth abide
          prowling the world
          and seeking the ruin of souls

this life leads to the cross

the world costs nothing
except your soul
                    but there are no
                    returns

NARRATIVE of SOJOURNER TRUTH; A Bondswoman of Olden Time, Emancipated by the New York Legislature in the Early Part of the Present Century: WITH A HISTORY OF HER LABORS AND CORRESPONDENCE DRAWN FROM HER "BOOK OF LIFE." BATTLE CREEK, MICH.: PUBLISHED FOR THE AUTHOR. 1878

one morning, she told Mrs. Van Wagener that her old master Dumont would come that day, and that she should go home with him on his return. They expressed some surprise, and asked her where she obtained her information. She replied, that no one had told her, but she felt that he would come.

It seemed to have been one of those 'events that cast their shadows before'; for, before night, Mr. Dumont made his appearance. She informed him of her intention to accompany him home. He answered, with a smile, 'I shall not take you back again; you ran away from me.' Thinking his manner contradicted his words, she did not feel repulsed, but made herself and child ready; and when her former master had seated himself in the open dearborn, she walked towards it, intending to place herself and child in the rear, and go with him. But, ere she reached the vehicle, she says that God revealed himself to her, with all the suddenness of a flash of lightning, showing her, 'in the twinkling of an eye, that he was *all over*'—that he pervaded the universe—'and that there was no place where God was not.' She became instantly conscious of her great sin in forgetting her almighty Friend and 'ever-present help in time of trouble.' All her unfulfilled promises arose before her, like a vexed sea whose waves run mountains high; and her soul, which seemed but one mass of lies, shrunk back aghast from the 'awful look' of him whom she had formerly talked to, as if he had been a being like herself; and she would now fain have hid herself in the bowels of the earth, to have escaped his dread presence. But she plainly saw there was no place, not even in hell, where he was not; and where could she flee? Another such 'a look,' as she expressed it, and she felt that she must be extinguished forever, even as one, with the breath of his mouth, 'blows out a lamp,' so that no spark remains.

A dire dread of annihilation now seized her, and she waited to see if, by 'another look,' she was to be stricken from existence—swallowed up, even as the fire licketh up the oil with which it comes in contact.

When at last the second look came not, and her attention was once more called to outward things, she observed her master had left, and exclaiming aloud, 'Oh, God, I did not know you were so big,' walked into the house, and made an effort to resume her work. But the workings of the inward man were too absorbing to admit of much attention to her avocations. She desired to talk to God, but her vileness utterly forbade it, and she was not able to prefer a petition. 'What!' said she, 'shall I lie again to God? I have told him nothing but lies; and shall I speak again, and tell another lie to God?' She could not; and now she began to wish for some one to speak to God for her. Then a space seemed opening between her and God, and she felt that if some one, who was worthy in the sight of heaven, would but plead *for* her in their own name, and not let God know it came from *her*, who was so unworthy, God might grant it. At length a friend appeared to stand between herself and an insulted Deity; and she felt as sensibly refreshed as when, on a hot day, an umbrella had been interposed between her scorching head and a burning sun. But who was this friend? became the next inquiry. Was it Deencia, who had so often befriended her? She looked at her, with her new power of sight—and, lo! she, too, seemed all 'bruises and putrifying sores,' like herself. No, it was some one very different from Deencia.

'Who *are* you?' she exclaimed, as the vision brightened into a form distinct, beaming with the beauty of holiness, and radiant with love. She then said, audibly addressing the mysterious visitant—'I *know* you, and I *don't* know you.' Meaning, 'You seem perfectly familiar; I feel that you not only love me, but that you always *have* loved me—yet I know you not—I cannot call you by name.' When she said, 'I know you,' the subject of the vision remained distinct and quiet. When she said, 'I don't know you,' it moved restlessly about, like agitated waters. So while she repeated, without intermission, 'I know you, I know you,' that the vision might remain—'Who are you?' was the cry of her heart, and her whole soul was in one deep prayer that this heavenly personage might be revealed to her, and remain with her. At length, after bending both soul and body with the intensity of this desire, till breath and strength seemed failing, and she could maintain her position no longer, an answer came to her, saying distinctly,

who do people say that i am?

    the baptist reborn
            elijah returned
                    a prophet new-coined

                    a deluded maniac

a judaized socratic figure
                    an occasion to collect popular folk wisdom sayings

a figurehead that serves to harmonize hellenic philosophy with a hesitant
but increasingly cosmopolitanizing jewish culture and which can then
reconcile the placidity of the roman multicultural civic religion with a
messianism that is the natural response of an oppressed underclass,
evacuating (and thereby alleviating) those anxieties into the dual heat-sinks
of a permanently forestalled soon-but-not-now eschatology and the
promise of an ameliorative and more just personal life to come

an apocalyptic preacher whose death and failed uprising was digested into
a suffering saviour narrative

                    a talented and charismatic pacifist faith healer
                    a proto-socialist revolutionary
                    an observant rabbi

a violent insurrectionist sanitized post-execution by surviving dissidents

an apostle turned splinter-sect of the truncated baptist purity cult

    the first creation of the father enfleshed

a refractive dimension of divine wisdom dispatched to save us from the
grotesqueries of the demiurge's material prison

    the pantocratic creative aspect of the triune god

        a gentle and domesticating peasant solar deity

        an aerosolization of a strand of first-century jewish ethics
following the cataclysm of the temple collapse

    you are the Christ

    oh

    what is that, exactly?

to follow me is to
        set your teeth
        upon the curb

kitsch coheres around the sublime like a barnacle
digesting it
parodying it

where there is beauty there is its tacky defective clone nearby
pressed from the excess extracted and distilled from it
          as if grace had a by-product
or the transcendent was an infection to be purged and
processed
cashiers souvenir stands money exchange security guard
slapping cameras down because the flash is bad for the
tincture and the rights to the image painted by cramping
hands in the workshops of the old masters have been sold
for an ad campaign

rimming the waterfalls like furious antibodies with tinsel
and tugboats freighted with raincoat gnomes and cascading
halogens that strobe the roar like spotlights nervous that the
unknown god might wake from its godzilla slumber

i watch you overturn tables of merchandise and open cages of birds that
flutter heavenward god knows how high
          escaping like helium balloons
          like the budgies we had when i was little getting themselves tangled
in a frantic bid through the plastic blinds hurling hollow bones against
glass that made me wonder if they truly hated us so much
          because the contours of cruelty are invisible to the jailer

          since the tomb in bethany when you woke me the wheels have come
off i guess and now you rage at the audacity and insolence and compromise

          of what after all are middlemen
          suffering their best under a regime and trying to service well-
meaning tourists who do not have the right change

          but patience and nuance
          were never really your strong suit
                    a typical capricorn i guess

(i wonder what happened to the whip? it'd make a great relic)

and pursued by ursine security guards
we exit through the gift shop

whoever leads others into captivity
will become themselves the captive

and whoever rises by the sword
will fall beneath its blade

let me remember you
let me understand you
let me love you

      increase only these and
      refashion me entirely

        —augustine of hippo

there was a woman i saw twice

when we returned home to capernaum from the decapolis it was clear
something had changed—word had gone out of your works, and now
jairus one of the same rich men who pushed you from the high places
clamoured by the boat begging favours

      master my daughter is dying. please come quick

and as we moved through the hugger-mugger throng a woman curled in
pain saw the celebrity healer pass and stretched out her hand. and brushed
your clothes
     who touched me
literally everyone, i said, it's a madhouse. but still you insisted
      i felt it. who touched me

stammering, terrified, she raised the offending hand as though you might
wither it.
she had been bleeding her whole life. it had left her bankrupt—
misdiagnosed, dismissed, embarrassed, in agony

      and i thought if i just touched the hem of his garments
          i could be made whole

and you smiled, and held her hand, and bid her peace. and she kept the
pickpocketed miracle. i saw her glassy-eyed and thankful as we hustled on

but now we were too late—the rich girl was dead
            (she got better, but)

i think i learned a little from that woman's audacity, and from your failure
      trapped in time even a god can run late
         and sometimes like jacob we must steal our blessings

years later in jerusalem amid the nightmare as i tried to push through
another desperate crowd my mind on fire following the hansel-gretel trail
of your gore as they marched you to the skull-place there she was again

      and i saw the woman who shoplifted a marvel had pressed a rag to
your face and held the print aloft like she was selling some grim line of
concert merch

an ugly, ghastly keepsake. a tacky souvenir. she was weeping, and her whole
life now radiant with meaning—a true icon
     this woman who had seen you once, heard half a sentence
       and understood you perhaps not at all

   with faith so much stronger than my own

michaelmas daisies among dead weeds
    blooming for michael's valorous deeds

and i beheld satan who is the devil fall as lightning
and crash-landing piss himself all over the last of the season's blackberries
    quite ruining the pie
            and outside the fields are white
            for harvest
            and the world goes into its sleep

but if today be bright and clear
    beware two winters fall this year

    let us remember the absent

my mother always feared that i would drown. watching me
cross-legged in front of cartoons learning my language and
whatever profit on it, making my father claw back a bid on a
house too close to the sea for fear i would plunge myself giddy
over its bluffs, buying a two-door instead of a four- when i
opened the handle during the test drive on the highway

i was skinny-dipping in the water on the spot i had once planned to kill
myself and still might, doing lazy laps from my father's boat at the opposite
quay and back, when i saw you sitting on the pier. i had left the house party
and you knew i was mad. at you and the girl who kept leaning on you.
and you did not reach down and pull me up next to you but watched me
scramble up the concrete, shivering and ungainly in the moonlight

       you couldn't help?

       you didn't ask

i sat next to you naked, you in your hoodie smelling of weed and me of the
moon. i felt my nakedness keenly but had as always with you to pretend
never to notice our locker room nudity. when you pulled off your wet
bathing suit or mooned me when you got off the couch, tugging on the
big ham hock of your thigh to wink your asshole at me the stout soft
udder of your cock dangling innocent below hair bristling halfway down
its length as i muttered fuck you and pushed you away. as blameless as a
horny dog, guiltless as adam in the garden of the laps to which you
consigned me with the other gym-faggots in the seventh circle while the
skies rain their fires, burning to see the underside of the beautiful
curvature of your balls or the hollow of your hip before the proud flare of
your fat round buttock

       why are you out here

       i wanted to see you

       what happened to what's her name

       come on. what you know that's not

and i felt even in the shiver of the night my cheeks get hot and i just asked,
finally

       how come you never kiss me when we're awake

and for a moment it was like i had slapped you, like i had smote the face of
god. and you looked at me, and i felt every bump and ripple of myself like
keen hot shame, sloshing like the water black below us

and from the half-disgorged pile of my kit you pulled an old blanket my grandmother had made of old rags and it was heavy and dense and should have been an heirloom but age and wear had degraded it into a beach throw. and you wrapped me in it, tightly, and it stank a little of the lake and you leaned in, and you put your soft warm mouth on mine, and waited for me to harden my lips into a kiss

and i was caught in thunder
scuttled in the tide of your breath

invective to Cerinthus, at the bathhouse

Cerinthus! hairspray heresiarch
    liar and teacher of lies

Cerinthus! effete and sniffling in the spa tepidarium
    complaining of the whiff of gentile smegma

        wearing a towel around his paunch
            and his t-shirt in the pool!

Cerinthus! who squealed in cloying cologne cloud that
    no man at all was Son of Man
    and instead blasphemed together a paper parade float
        cheap chaste hologram apollo
        quivering castrati of the choir, warbling dim hallelujahs
            for a holy infant idiot
            tender and mild

Cerinthus! who would make a virgin of both god and me!
    Cerinthus! the face i catch in a rococo mirror
        darkly

    go back to your ablutions, million mom marching
    Cerinthus
    rinse your hamster balls in chlorine till the raid

    unwashed i'll go home reeking
    i have god's donkey dick to suck

    and let the light that lit the stars
        bathe my cleft clean with his tongue

after browning

a stick, once fire from end to end
    now ashes
    save the tip that holds a spark

yet blow

    and taste again the truth of things

who saw, and heard, and could remember all

        head wool-white, eyes flame, and feet like brass
sword and seven stars

how did I bear that sight and live?

        [and] when [I] scatter, there is left on earth
no one alive who knew
        saw with his eyes and handled with his hands
that which was from the first, the Word of Life

how will it be when none more saith "I saw"?

    I saw, I heard, I knew
grasping the while for stays at facts which snap

    wear the thickness thin, and let man see
with me, who hardly am withheld at all

let us love one another
      for love is of God
      for God is nothing else but love

      if the perfect God can climb down from the throne and into the mud
      then the mud of us too is sacred
            filled with his breath
            quickened by the warmth of his hand
            washed and mingled with his blood

if even God can die then death is no indignity
      if even God can love then love can be no sin

and if God so loved us
      loved me

      then beloved we ought also to love one another

      and so love fearlessly
            dwell in love
            dwell in him
            because he first loved us

TOO LOUD
TOO BRIGHT TOO HOT

volume at maximum
across all visible spectra
like a cat walking across the keys of creation

you stand atop the crag
unfolding
disclosing the toxic light of theophany
the math of reality ripped apart and nullified

     common to both going apart coming together raised up
     on high dancing [vox nihili] of three signs like in kind [vox nihili]

     my brother and peter and i cling to the rock cling to our own atoms
as you take off the raiment of yourself and the static crackles across the
skin of creation and next to you are two figures one is moses one is elijah
(how do i know one is moses and one is elijah?) and somehow *peter* is
speaking?? shouting to the braising maelstrom

     master do you need some . . . tents??? for your friends???

and a voice like a garbage truck like a mic squeal like my mother's softest
lullaby like my own voice said

     THIS IS MY SON. LISTEN TO HIM

     and then: all the world goes dead, like the plug yanked from
     the wall socket of a vacuum cathode tv and gravity returns
     to earth standard and our corneas stop blistering

and you sneeze
and shake like a wet labrador

    well
    that was fun

i am the alpha and omega
      the beginning and the end
            the first and the last

            root of the offspring of david
            the bright and ascendant morning star

i am thy fellow servant

on the first of september after i finished making dinner i asked her if she'd like to go for a walk. and we clamped the footrests into her wheelchair and we went backwards over the bump of the driveway and i watched the wind with a chill in it move through her thinning hair and she tugged my sleeve to whisper

it's getting cold

yes, i said. do you want to go back?

no, she said
this is probably my last one

and i felt the rivet of this. and i pushed her by the little paved walkway by the creek and a mourning dove took flight in panic from us and she asked why all the birds were quiet and i said they had all made their nests and raised their babies but then i heard two hooded warblers

look there, on top of the pine tree

but it hurt her head too much to look

and at the top of the footbridge over the creek just near where the highway bisects the town into north and south she asked me to stop. and she peered through the rusting grate at the water gliding past us both towards the wide grey of the winter

for there are three that witness [in heaven

the father
the word
the holy spirit

      and these three are one

and there are three that witness on earth]

the spirit
the water
the blood

      and these three are one

i know thy works
that thou art neither cold nor hot

        so then because thou art lukewarm
        i will spew thee from my mouth

and before the throne the seven angels began to sound their trumpets

    and from the sky fell horrors

devouring the green
curdling the sea
souring the waters

and i saw a great star fall
    burning as a lamp

    [and the name of the star is Wormwood]

and its poison flowed through all the waters of the earth

and a third of creation was marred
and a third of heaven was swallowed in darkness

the sun smitten
and the moon dimmed
    and chaos and old night overcame the stars

the cashier, a young handsome italian in a cute little visor and apron, warns me in a thick accent "be careful there are a lot of smarties!" as i take the mcflurry from him and i have just enough time to wonder why would i need a warning about smarties before i send two tablespoons of smarties skittering across the floor

"i warned you!" he crows in dismay
i am forever disappointing beautiful men, a sky full of asterized antinouses creasing their perfect brows as i drop ice cream cones across the ages

as the industrial air conditioner chills to freezing the sweat of my forehead and my saturated pits i crunch ice-milk and candy sediment like the concrete of a collapsed mosaic as in the square the fountain burbles and burps with the disgusting rude allure that is the privilege of every thing of beauty

it is july in rome and from the mcdonald's in the piazza della rotonda through the endless thunk and shud of its automatic doors opening and closing like a vaseline lid to barf out a blast of cold i watch the sightsers stop and start into hadrian's mighty pantheon

the plaza is one of the quiet achievements of the baroque, the sweep and the scoops of its waterworks made by the volatile hands of bernini and della porta and barigioni, then crowned at its height with a glory pulled from the papal *wunderkammer*: a red sharp marble obelisk, jutting from the city like a bone spur

> as a style the baroque specialized in setting precious stones and objects, the captive treasures of the civilizing catholicizing colonializing world—ostrich eggs and coconut husks and avocado cores encased by hyperactively enthusiastic jewellers in spiralling vertiginous gilt

this crimson pillar, tooth of a long-dead crocodile divinity, is the salvage of empire—raised by ramses the great in heliopolis to praise the sun god ra. after his slaves had all fled across a bisected sea, the stone was then dragged from the nile to rome to be a maypole for isis. when those revels too were ended, it was tipped into the mud, and the delving renaissance popes found it dumped beneath an apse. they capped it, with their usual shrewd syncretism, with a little tin crucifix like a barn weathervane and set it for another few centuries to stab at the sun

now a little girl dunks her spongebob in the font in the same long shadow where moses slew a slaver

gaze upon my works ye mighty

two men will be in the field
one will be taken
and the other left

two women grinding at the mill
one will be taken
and the other left

and i saw a star fall
streaking from heaven
     and to this fallen was given the key to the bottomless pit

     and he opened the pit
and the smoke of its furnace blotted out the sun

     and from that smoke locusts swarmed
          and their torment was as the torment of a scorpion

     and in those days shall men seek death
     and they shall not find it

it occurs to me keats died coughing not far away, hacking polite spatters of
blood onto linen squares like sonnets. i wonder if he knew he passed one
of grim ozymandias's works every day on his way to morning coffee

what did we all come to this desert to find?

i cross the lone and level stretch of the hot piazza and clad in dirty
birkenstocks break the threshold of the all-shrine

in the eye of the pantheon
in the thick sunlight shaft of the temple's oculus
the dust motes sing hymns to lucretius
a world crumbled out into atomies
all in pieces
all coherence gone

a caravaggio universe catching tax collectors and vacationing
stockbrokers in chiaroscuro denunciations
its studded honeycomb is the "santa maria ad martyres" now but the vault
and vat of its strafing twilight remembers older gods:

its apostate light once fell on venus
bedecked in pearls lent to her by cleopatra
a great barocco halved for each of her stone-deaf ears

here the bones and ashes of raphael, reluctantly affianced, are smothered
in incense beside his unwelcome almost bride

and the glittering bronze of its dome
that once caught the evening light and set the tiber aflame
the scurrying popes melted long ago for their cannons

the barberinis accomplishing what the barbarian could not

this is not a place of honour
no gods live here
it is a dwelling place of corpses a
reef of coralizing shipwreck faiths
this is the tomb of empires
boundless and bare

why do you look for the living among the dead?

amid the gawking tour groups craning at a lifeless god's magnificent eye i
remember:

a hovel in capernaum
the only shade from a noontime sun packed to its rafters blocking every
door with people listening to you speak

and your laughter
            like living water
as the plank and plaster of the ceiling began above us to crumble and fall
in sheets, pulled apart by many hands

        and through the rough aperture a group of boys lowered their young
    stricken friend's cot from the bright hole they had pushed like a wrecking
                                                    ball through the sky

            just so you could make him whole again

you know what you all remind me of?
you're like a gaggle of kids in the market

        critiquing everyone who comes along
        whining one isn't chipper enough
            and should really smile more
        that another isn't as respectful
           or sombre as you'd like

meanwhile there's still fucking work to do

and i heard a new song

      and all the earth was harvested
            fruit for the vintner
      and the winepress was trod
      and from the winepress teemed a vintage of blood

and from the seven angels poured seven vials

      pouring forth sores upon the wicked
      pouring forth blood into the sea
      pouring forth gore into the rivers
      pouring forth heat into the sun
      pouring forth darkness on the blasphemous
      pouring forth hordes out of the wastes

and the last angel at the field of armageddon
      pouring forth the end

let me be a heretic
       and break the doctrine of imperfect creeds

let me be a blasphemer
       and spit in the face of all gods dead and dim

let me be a sorcerer
       and put my hand to knowledges
       and technologies forbid

let me be an apostate
       and leave behind the faiths that bind me

let me be a vandal
       and deface what should be faceless

let sacrilege and desecration reign
       where treasures are stored
       there is hidden your heart

       let every temple fall

       that which can be destroyed
       must be destroyed

       and what he will raise again will quicken
       transformed
              in three days
              in a twinkling

       the old things pass away
       to make all things anew

i will know no allegiance but love

[an elaborate yet oddly elegant time paradox is unfolded by the Creator that is planimetrically consonant with the entire unfolding action of cosmic history itself: God crowns the Son because God foreknows the Son will one day redeem the fall that enmity for his crown causes. Cause and effect collapse into a singularity: Satan fell because God elevated the Son, and/but God elevated the Son because Satan fell]

[God, perfect and entire, unfolds from his perfection a system, into which a complicating variance is introduced. This variance introduces a repeating, sophisticating, and unending fractalizing pattern. All of cosmic history, space and time, unfurls along this principle of introducing generative asymmetries, its entire plot warping and bending around the impossible paradox of the Son, who bisects the face of its entire timeline: the first cause and final resolution of all its problems, the first expression of ineffability from which all other expression flows and the millennial fulfillment of its homeward return]

Meanwhile
The world shall burn, and from her ashes spring
New heaven and earth, wherein the just shall dwell
And after all their tribulations long
See golden days, fruitful of golden deeds,
With joy and love triumphing, and fair truth.
Then thou thy regal sceptre shalt lay by,
For regal sceptre then no more shall need,
God shall be all in all.

[God will, it seems, evacuate the centre; he abdicates and abnegates, installing his Son (flung haphazardly into history, marred, scarred flesh and all) as his vice-regent: God's throne is to be empty. For his asymmetric artwork of creation to be completed, God recognizes he must exit its frame via his own abdication, an eliminating of any last semblance of a controlling, authorizing architect, and an annihilative dissolve into the sublime plenitude of his own creation]

[the great wonderwork of creation is to evacuate finally its originary point entirely, leaving a hollow centre, its sophisticated, propagating system of hierarchies and declensions without any guarantee or stabilizing nexus. The baroque God who made worlds within worlds out of his own body shall be all in all with no centralizing axis of rotation]

[yet the note the retiring deity strikes is not of closure or threnodic elegy, but open-ended vatic delight at new possibilities and feats that he himself seems only dimly to be able to imagine or perceive: golden days, fruitful of golden deeds]

and i saw the lamb open the sixth seal

and:

      the earth shuddered
      the sun winked black
      the moon poured blood

      and i saw the stars drop to the earth
          like figs shaken by the wind

      and i saw the depleted sky peel back like a scroll
      and every isle and mountain fall

      and the kings
      and the great
      and the rich
      and the mighty
      and the wise
      and the servant
      and the slave
      and the free

      hid themselves in caves and bunkers
          and begged the mountains hide them

      for the wrath of the lamb is come
          and who shall be able to stand?

and i saw no temple
city of no sun, neither of the moon
this is the day that the lord's unmade
let us rejoice and be glad
hosanna in the highest heights!

as ticking clock breaks silence with its chime
as hill unbowed cracks down to foaming sea
as forlorn goddess racks and withers clime
so do i wreck my hours with thoughts of thee

on wasted days, on nights that spilled to morn
till misspent week to months to years are grown
and knowing all i loved, i loved alone

and i had seen the sun at stop
[beholding distant dawns with beams unshorn]
rose and thorn
forewarn
scorn
bemourn
reborn

and you broke the bread and shared it with all of them, and you said:

> i am bread
> broken to be fed upon

and you passed the wine to each and said:

> i am wine
> guzzled to slake ancient thirst

and you said:

> when you gather
> when you eat
> when you laugh
> remember me
> i am there

and you said:

> i will be betrayed
> i will be denied

but they said:

> master
> what about him
> whom you hold to your chest
> whom you dandle in your arms?
>
> you have said we all must suffer
> you have said we all must die
> what of him?

and you said:

> some are here who will not taste death
> till i return
>
> if he should live till i come again in glory
> what is that to you?

[i am at the sink helping my mother clean fish,
the stainless steel and their narrow silvers a universe of
mercury and throbbing purpled under her rough nail.
reaching under the gills to rip out their guts as at the
kitchen table my dad yells bloviations into the phone.
your grandfather would get mad if you broke their necks
she tells me into a sink of red and i try to imagine the old
rugged whaler who could not read or cook as pepper and
salt join the squish the gush the glop the gulp. a
hundred mouths distend their cartilage as roan sac and
tube sing their dark hosanna. family is just this it is
sharing joyful death]

you look to earth and sky and glean the coming storm
now look to here and now and see
what is to come

Christus, the founder of the name, underwent the death penalty in the reign
of Tiberius, by sentence of the procurator Pontius Pilate, and for a moment
the pernicious superstition was checked.

—Annals of Tacitus

pilate they say was a suicide, sunk beneath the tiber, and
haunts the cold lake of his waterlogged corpse in high
mountain passes, swooping down like a revenant raising
tempests. and they are fond of crafting special hells for
caiaphas—dante leaves him drowning in effluvia, nailed to
the highway, pavement trod by hypocrites untold
i had met caiaphas many times. elbowed my way into the
courts with peter, trading every bit of cultural coin i had
gained in my stay with the leper just to squat by the
servant's fire and listen to peter's whimpering twilit
apostasies. amazing what fear can do. and when we preached
in the city, long after caiaphas brought peter and me again
before him and begged us to be silent. to think of the
people. to think of rome. his thinking i guess was not so
different than god's: let one man die so others are saved. the
needs of the many against the few
these councils, these conspiracies, these kings—thoughtful,
sober, anxious for their offices, perplexed in their devotions.
when i saw their eyes dart, for all their jewellery and pomp, it
was worry not malice that i saw
small, complicated, complicit men, faced with would-be
messiahs daily, attempting to forestall the calamity that did
indeed come after him, and which (not miraculously, but
with the shrewdness of any who could see the coming
weather) he had foreseen
they saw a popular following. they saw a demonstrable
contempt for the uneasy peace of the occupation and its
thousand compromises and concessions. they saw he had

ridden in triumph with a crowd waving fronds at his back
into the tinderbox of the capital, the ensigns and gonfalons
of rome swirling scarlet in the temple courts
it matters that the powers of the state killed him. that by
the lights of law and loyalty they were right to do so. he
spoke against empire and capital and capitulation. the
things they said he said he said the things they said he did
he did. he came to break apart their world; you would have
killed him too

the master died a traitor
and a terrorist

                    take up your cross
                    and follow fast behind him

once there was a woman with ten coins
        who lost one

    and she tore her house apart
        closet disgorged
        drawers pulled out

    till she found it

and once there was a shepherd with a hundred sheep
    and one wandered away

        and he left the ninety-nine
        and ranged over hill and dale

    till he found him in a bramble

    and brought him home singing on his shoulders

no one blames the coin or sheep
    misplaced in the dust
    lost in the woods

    but know: someone is looking
    the search party seeks
    and god will tear the universe
        shred the law
        abolish gravity and constancy and flesh
        to deliver you safe

    a miracle is the sound of reality buckling

    i love you
    and

        if i lost you
        there is nowhere i wouldn't look

    and

        if i found you
        there would be no end to my rejoicing

there was a time you knew each inch of me
kissed my fingers after chopping garlic and onions
darted your tongue between sandy toes
        behind my ear, licking lint from my belly
or tasted my armpits in deep, furious lapping
        your frantic kisses tasting of my deodorant
and afterwards
your mouth against my brokenness
        savouring the froth
        like a cat lapping cream

        now the still softness of me is gone
        the wood that once was emerald grown dried to kindling
        and on my skin you would read scars of strange provenance

        and i wonder now if you came back
        if i could forgive your immortality

        and you my dwindling

when you pray, say only this:

      god is our father

      we honour him as our source and caregiver

      we work to build a world worthy to inherit
             to make ourselves skilled and careful instruments

      we ask for what we need to get us through today
             and accept tomorrow is not ours to worry about

      we ask our failures be forgiven us
             as we work to forgive those who have failed us

      we ask to be released from harm
             that is past and that is to come
             from without and from within

                          Amen

to be near me
is to be near a fire

we moved through a field of sunflowers, idiot faces heavy, laden with seed, grinning with a thousand ugly joyful teeth at us as we moved among their stalks stretching to the horizon. swelling and dilating for the harvest

and the traitor a consummate grad student following with us said:

> every day the sunflower offers its face to the sun
> it cannot choose else

> alone among all the good things planted in the garden, we only can turn and look another way

> how marvellous to be an automaton adam
> an electronic eve
> executing uncorrupted and incorruptible code

i looked at you and you pinched my thumb and stuck out your tongue and i swelled again with light

> imagine a dad gave a bunch of money to his children
>> he wants them to invest it, spend it, waste it, increase it
>> enjoy it

>> show him the world as they would make it
>> not just bury it in the dirt

> how sad if god was as good as it gets
>> an artist whose work could not exceed himself

>> a father who would praise a fugitive and cloistered virtue
>>> won without dust and heat
>> does not sound very familiar to me
>>> god loves most of all what is broken

>>> for if our father valued perfection above all he
> wouldn't have made anything at all
>>> he already had that
>>> perfection is just a place to start

> instead imagine wondrous variety
>> infinite diversity in infinite combinations

>> imagine a god you could impress and
>>> surprise him

>> sing a new song unto the lord

i will come
as a thief in the night

don't let me find you sleeping

as we walked some of us began to glean from the field
cracking seeds as we went

but there were some there who grew distressed
       because it was the day of rest
       and this was not our field to glean

you sighed

           the sun does not stop for the sabbath

           life is for the enjoying
           instead you fast at a wedding

               and even the days of rest you turn into a chore

and you said:

           don't you know what david did when he and his men were
hungry?
           he entered the house of the high priest
           and they all ate up the consecrated bread
           which only the priests could eat

and they said: that's not technically what happens in that story

and you said:

           oh well

           i guess i stole that too

what parent among you

    if asked for a fish
    would give your child a snake

    if asked for an egg
    would give your child a scorpion

       the sparrow
             does not worry for the harvest
      and the flower
             though clothed in splendour
            does not sew

i promise you if you will learn it:

     there is enough
          too much
    for you and for all

       and you will be ok

a rich young man came to him and said: good teacher

oh i'm nothing special

what must i do to inherit eternal life?

      the usual ten commandment stuff
            don't murder, don't cheat on your partner, you know
            the code of hammurabi is basically the same
            honestly most ethical systems end up pretty similar

      you don't need me for that part

but i've always done that
how do i follow you?

            oh in that case
            you only have to do one thing
            go
            sell all you have

            there's no such thing as a rich Christian

and the youth was very sad
because he had inherited much
and was only growing richer

      who then can possibly be saved?

and he shrugged

            i don't know what to tell you

            how can anyone wealthy
            claim to be good?

you stand almost in the surf, the raging red bull pushed back nearly into the unicorn sea, facing the conflagration and the mob firelit and frenzied

on the cliffs behind us all of magdala is burning, and the romans' horses are dead. they drag me to the shore past the heap of them in the stables, throats cut gouting on the ground. now they fling me at your feet, upon the sand of the beach, pulled from bed, arm still in its cast: faggot fuel for the witch's fire

when you arrived, rushing through her house to scoop me up, my brother had asked you to destroy this town for what it had done to us. to me. and part of me, the son of thunder in me, had wanted lightning to flicker in your eyes and for you to have smitten this sleepy village with a fist from heaven for raising its hand to your darling. now it is burning and i choke on ash and shame to have made so mean a wish. i wonder if the zealot started the fire, but in the crowd i don't see any of us. just leering horrors, the sun setting crimson above the bluffs

she is standing, unashamed. they have taken her clothes to expose her but she hides nothing. and from the crowd a snarl:

> this mismatched masterpiece of confusion
> > has made itself the catamite of rome
> > has prostituted itself to our oppressors
> > caught in the act of adultery and worse

> the law says it must be stoned

you spare me a glance and must see the terror there. there is no way out of this. and meet in her gaze the dignity i can never seem to summon

> let he who is without sin
> be first to throw his stone

then in the sand of the beach you stoop and begin to write. and i hear rocks drop, thudding wetly, one by one

by nightfall there are only three of us. you give her your cloak, and she slaps you, hard and strong, and the sound breaks like a wingbeat

and from the crags we watch the tide rinse the beach clean of what you scrawled in the sand

the only gospel you ever wrote
all the words you might have said
by the breakers
    washed and gone

and he shall wipe every tear from every eye

and there shall be no more death
                    neither sorrow
                    nor crying
neither shall there be any more pain

        for the old things are passed away

                and behold:

                i make all things new

and he fed a crowd of four thousand (which was smaller) and again there were leftovers to send home with the crowd of seven baskets full (which was less)

and as we were packing up a group came to him demanding a sign, and he groaned

> why does everyone want a sign?
> no generation understands the time it lives in
>
>> no one sees the miracles they trip through
> so no: no sign today sorry

and we got in the boat, and he sat in its stern, butting his thick eyebrow caterpillars together and fulminating like a storm grumping at the coast

the vibe was terrible

it was around this time that peter sheepishly confided he had forgotten to keep any of the leftovers, and we only had one loaf of bread to eat in the boat

and then suddenly he said:

> beware the leaven of cynics

and peter, who means really well all the time but could be a little slow with a metaphor, made a sheesh with his face and said "oh no—he's mad we don't have any bread"

but even though peter was quiet, he heard it in that usual way of his

> how could you think i meant actual bread
> you have seen literally miracle after miracle
>
> i just
>> why do i bother

and he folded up, and went to sleep

> and like ok i get it
> but honestly i do think at least part of it was that he was hungry

through eternity you were
        you are
        and you will be

but if past is different from future
        and present is different from past and from future
        how can your eternity exist always as a whole?

does none of your eternity pass by
        so that it no longer is
        and does none of it become what, so to speak, it is not yet?

then: you were not yesterday and will not be tomorrow
        instead, yesterday, today, and tomorrow, you are
        you simply are—existing beyond time

you do not exist yesterday or today or tomorrow
        for yesterday, today, and tomorrow
        are nothing other than worldly distinctions

so, although without you nothing can exist
        you are not in space or time
but all things are in you

        and so
        you are not contained by anything
        rather you contain all things

                —anselm of canterbury

i watch thomas shove his filthy faithless merchant finger into the ragged
hole they've made in your side
a salmon slab assessed at discount as other tarped stalls close with a rattle
      a grisly teeth-checking show-and-tell
      dyspeptic didymus buying meat for cheap

and i remember
waking up on a morning impossibly bright after we had closed the bar
together, the thick white snow swirling upwards outside the ninth-floor
window, and you
      face down, asleep and snoring in rhotics like a boat's motor
         the tangle of your hair tumbling over your eyes full of sand
and matted to your damp brow (you always ran too hot even in winter)
         the sheets peeled off you in characteristic tantrum, crinkled
white duvet and soft acrylic shush of my mother's crochet resting below
the astonishing perfect plush of your backside
      buttocks dusted with fur caught in the cockcrow light
         peach fuzz shimmering like theodora's halo rimmed in saffron

      and i remember running the saddle of my thumb down the small of
your back tracing the dark black cowlick whorl there and then with
uncharacteristic daring down the fault-line and
in whisper-light soft circles around soft velvet
watching you smile before your eyes wake then crinkling bashfully
      i haven't showered

      and begging forgiveness i began to press earnestly against
         the firm bud knot that shyly ties you shut

      and a small intake of breath at my ear, and you folding, and whining,
just a little, and butting your head gently into mine and mashing the wet of
your mouth against my neck
      throwing the bulk of your heavy leg over my waist like a tree trunk
falling on forest bed, gripping my head and back, jamming your big knee
under my flexing arm as it worked
               the spiced musk of you incensing the air
        shaking in plumes, dripping like sap from your half-limp dick as
            heavenly fragrance fills the circuit wide
              of cassia, nard, and balm

as my thumb presses against your firming core underside and my
middle finger sinks slowly
      past the perfect supple aperture of your untightening
      slipping down to bump of beckoning knuckle

now radiant resplendent and renewed
i wonder if up close you even smell the same

do you want credit for loving those who love you?
do you only do good to those who are good to you?
do you only lend money to people who are good for it?

      so what
      even reprobates do that

      instead:

love your enemies
be kind to those who hate you
and lend without ever being repaid

      be merciful
      as your father is merciful

i am in the kitchen late at night oiling an old
wooden cutting board when i see them: five
or six bright pink dots on its surface,
stubbornly refusing to move or smudge

and peering at them i remember suddenly:
sitting on the couch watching television and
his cellphone is ringing and he untangles
from me an elbowed octopus of right angles
in a frantic call he writes on a sticky note
with a neon marker and it bleeds through (as
i know, in my august wisdom, it will) and he
tries to wipe it and then looks up in quiet
adorable panic to see if i notice and i pretend
i do not and he never mentions it, not once,
the little shit

and i finish oiling the board in soft circles,
and set it by the sink, and the apartment
which was always too small for both of us
echoes a sound i cannot hear

the people were watching us eat and they said to him:

your followers are disgusting

they do not wash their hands
they defile their bodies

with tattoos and mutilations
with gorging and starving
with drug and drink

and he said:

i want you to understand this
because apparently it is still unclear to you:

the body is never the index of sin
aesthetics are never ethics
and illness is never iniquity

defilement is something you do
not ingest

thus he declared all things of the body clean

and i beheld a spirit come down from heaven
    clothed in a cloud
    crowned with the iris
        his face as the sun
        his feet as fire

and he bestrid the narrow world as a colossus
    a foot upon the sea
    a foot upon the land
        and i stood beneath him

and from a scroll he spoke words to me
    words to end the world
    words that should finish the mysteries of god
    but then said:

    do not write them
        they are for you alone

and i took the scroll that was in his hand
    and he said:

            take it
            eat it up

    taste its taste as sweet as honey
    feel your belly made full sore

and i took the scroll of him into me

    and his taste was sweet as honey in my mouth
        and my belly was made sore

    and after he did this he said to me:

    you will be my testament
    before peoples nations tongues and kings

one night I felt myself linger while
we cleaned the bar polishing the
spigots of the soda syrups wiping
down the espresso machine and he
kissed me quick and fast my ass
against the chrome of the ice well
and instead of hot I felt a rush of
coldness like a plunge into a cave
grotto and unbidden I felt my cock
ooze precum spotting my clothes
through to outside as above us in
the purple the disco ball spun and
the sound system belched eighties
soundtracks pop songs about the
autobot matrix of leadership and
passersby cheered and hooted at us
through the glass

only the servant knows
how to justly rule

not: if you're not with us, you're against us
but: if you're not against us, you're with us

let them talk and theorize and fight with you
        and hear words and words and words

        know your ally by this:
                who fills your thirsty cup

spice left unseasoned becomes dust
salt left unsprinkled becomes stale

break open every storehouse
pour profusion on the earth
be generous, be zest
be living fire and

        use all you can
        while you can

a woman in labour is sorrowful that her time has come
but when the child is born she forgets her anguish

       someday there will be happiness again
       and a joy that none can take from us

let us be the bread of life
that together we may never hunger
that together we may never thirst

there is a life i should have had:

swelling to paunchy manhood, bespectacled, respectable, inheriting
my father's dingy dinged-up storefront clotted with fresh paint and
capturing some poor wife, tugging you off furtively balding on
weekends in the den our kids on shitty soccer teams together
chasing errant underinflated balls and populating upstairs rooms
with suspended solar system grandchildren for my doting mother
as frailty spiderwebs all through her and her tongue thickens and
stops while my dad rattles senescent curses in the garage

my parents could have both died quietly and proud of me

we would be dead
burying the dead

i know
i just wanted to say it out loud

if your hand offends you, cut it off
    better to be whole
    with one hand

if your eye offends you, pluck it out
    better to be whole
    with one eye

if your foot offends you, cut it off
    better to be whole
    with one foot

    be perfect
    as god is perfect

    be wounded
    as god is wounded

the opposite of hell
is a scar

you and i across from each other, in the hot scented water of the
magdalene's massive clawfoot. i can feel the soak of it pulling soreness
from my bruises and tenderized side like balm. the water is brimful and
milky with her salts and soaps and spiderwort petals floating on its top.
from a dorm-sized fridge in her room she has also given us a bottle of very
sweet, very cold moscato and plunked it in a green beach pail full of ice,
and i am pouting

>   i feel bad. this feels expensive

>   oh come on. you can have a nice thing
>   if you want all dirt all the time you can always go eat bugs in the
>   desert with my cousin

you have styled your hair into a soapy stegosaurus ridge and are dragging
from a joint, which you balance in a soapdish on the tub's lip next to a
plastic champagne flute with a snap-together base. out of place in the
bathroom's pinks and fluff, like a hairy satyr snuck into a bower

with one foot pressed flat against the tile next to my head and the other in
my crotch you look at me for a moment through the rising steam and i am
not sure if it is a tiger or a deer that is lapping across the water. which of
us has tamed which

>   we can be dirty socialists and sleep in a ditch again tomorrow. just
>   rinse the road out of your cute little crack

>   it still feels wrong

for a moment you are almost pouting, as though i am on the verge of
ruining some occasion whose contours i have forgotten

>   i promise there will still be plenty of poor people when i'm gone

your old fatalism hits me in the stomach worse than the frat boy punches.
i feel the tears rise from some depth i didn't expect. delayed panic from
the crowd maybe, or the aching body-stress of my broken arm, or just
missing you. how strange—it had only been a week or two. and now it
yawns to centuries

>   don't say that. what? it's true

as a sob escapes you huff your long guttural huff, forever exhausted at the universe's insufficiencies. when i forget your voice i just listen across the years for the huff

and you spin on your butt with a squeal against the porcelain, hurtling water recklessly splashing over the lip of the tub to soak the clothes shucked around it, and pull me into a nursing hug

> shh
> my little guy
> don't worry

you pour a handful of sudsy water over my head and kiss my brow and rest your stippled jaw there, which is very sweet, and then i feel you gently start rummaging around between my thighs under the water which is less sweet, cupping your hand underneath me pushing against the port to test the watertightness of the seal there and oh [ephphatha! which is, be opened!]

you press your forehead against mine, cheap sweet wine on your breath, joint still in your teeth, and grin a crooked haphazard grin. teeth white as sheep

i turn to find your big, stupid mouth a last rough male thing a hardness amid all the liquid eucalyptus smoothness of the oils and unguents and salves, our fingers linked

> beware: the wrath of the lamb

> you think you're just incredibly funny

> i am that i am

> just try not to pee in the pool for once

> hey wait. listen seriously this is important shh listen

the softball-sized bubble of your fart bursts the surface of the water like a trumpeting elephant

> i hate you so much

> put that in red letters bitch

holding ever my right hand, the lord
led me to sit upon his empty throne.
then he fitted on my finger a golden
ring

    may this ring be a token of our
    love. you are mine, and i am
    yours

    my honour is yours; your
    honour is mine

        i will be your husband
and   you will be my husband

   all that is mine is yours, and all
        that is yours is mine

and what i am by nature you will share by grace

    and so, forever

    you and i are one

   —the vision of blessed bernardo de hoyos
       translated from the spanish

oh that I knew how all thy lights combine,
and the configurations of their glory!
seeing not only how each verse doth shine,
but all the constellations of the story

—george herbert

in the fairy tales some impossible
                 sad task, and hard is set

        if psyche winnows the corn of the sacrifice
        if cinderella picks the lentils from the ashes
        if david piles the floor with foreskins of the philistines

        if i make a cambric shirt
                        without seam or needlework
        to replace the one they stole
        casting dice at your pierced and beautiful feet like bronze
        if i stitch a thousand years, darting back and looping
        somewhere i will find the slipped knot and set it right

because if you are very very good and diligent and patient
the god returns to you
                merciful and kind and proud of your faithfulness
                it was only a test lois
                and you get your wish

and then you'll come back to me
                and i'll be forgiven my insolence
                        for daring to touch the staff of your godhood
                        for letting my belly swell with you
                        for spilling hot oil upon your perfect chest

        back asleep in your arms
                        folded in your wings
                        happily ever after

        yesterday grows merry in time

but in my garden as i age and sage eccentric blossoms grow
        the grain i sort germinates and roots before i am done the count
        the sickle you gave me for harvest rusts and crackles
        and crows fall greedy upon kernels yet uncounted and unparsed
        as the crocus chirps and the grackle blooms

        the centuries grow rank and go to seed
        i find my mind quite overgrown

and my memories and my verses sprout strange herbs
    parsley sage grows merry and thyme
        like an arcimboldo
        a vegetable king forgetting forgotten
sing me a song of a lad that is gone

        how long must i wait for you
        too long at the fair

on your resplendent throne in the fourfold sky
        as the empyreal vault grinds another granite turn
        and the sober millennium spins its gears
        cycle and epicycle, orb in orb

i wonder if you ever think of me:
        sampling the blueberry cheesecake ripple
        with every intention of the pistachio scoop

hip-checking you at the sink
        so i can spit out my mouthwash

        or snuggling into bed
        my cold feet raising a shout

        trying to steal a little
        of your cozy cherub warmth

dark night of the soul
saint juan de la cruz
translated from the spanish

in the dark
anxious and ardent for love
    —oh happy flight!—
i snuck unseen
from my silent house

stolen secret and sheltered
down the disused stairs
    —oh happy flight!—
muffled among the shadows
from my silent house

in the blissful night
in secret, unseen
and unseeing
with no other guide or light
but my desperate heart

this hidden fire will guide me
more certain than the sun at noon
to where you wait for me
who i know so well
where we will be unseen

oh night that led me on!
night more kindly than the dawn
night that joins
lover with beloved
and beloved with lover
till each becomes the other

and cradled in my thrumming
breast
that is his and his alone
there he dozed
as i caressed
him in the cedared breeze

wind blew from the battlement
as i ran my hand through his hair
it stung my neck
with gentleness
and all my senses stopped

and so i remained, lost and
oblivious
my face reclined against my
beloved
all ceased, i abandoned myself
leaving my cares
forgotten in the lilies

when i was a kid my mom used to tell me a story:

once upon a time
there was a boy king
and he was very brave and kind
but he fought in a terrible war

     against who

honestly no idea
realistically it would be probably
like
problematic to look into, considering
anyway
they said he fell in battle
in the dust with all his armour
trampled by the horses
and with him the whole kingdom fell
and it never recovered

but see my mom said he didn't really die
he was only asleep
and on some days in the mist where she grew up
you could see the island across the water
where he was sleeping

and he'd come back again someday

i asked her about it the other day
but
she didn't even remember telling me
and he probably wasn't really a good dude at all
but i used to think about it all the time

     why are you telling me this

it's just
what if you went away for a while

       like the boy king
       or are you supposed to be the

no i mean
what if you weren't
in danger

      are you
      you're not trying to get rid of me

this isn't going to end well
for me
for any of us

but you could be safe
you could go somewhere safe
and i could stay away
and when i was gone
at least i'd know

i don't mind dying
i was born to die
but you

if you should live until i come again
      what is that to anyone?

      you can't protect me from the world

oh
yes i can
watch me
just watch me

and he kissed where
worry creased my forehead
and both lingered there till sleep

he has no body now on earth but yours
no hands but yours
no feet but yours

yours must be the eyes now
which regard the world
with compassion

yours must be the feet now
which set about
with errand

yours must be the hands now
which reach out
with blessing

lying on the futon in your filthy dorm room windowless
the scratch of occasional cockroaches from the restaurant below
(once i caught one under a glass and named it cs lewis and you
were mad as it skritched against the coaster) with a greasy pizza
box on the floor half-eaten
as the dvd loops the same thirty-second music cue from *Psycho* and
suddenly you have pulled me into a straddle and

oh
you peel my shorts from me and slide past and through and i cry out and
wonder at last if god hates fags just a little as you tear through me like a lance
to bathe my heart in the hot gushed fountain of your seed in short, sharp
shock in jabs like a bee tearing itself loose from the organs and apparatus
of its stinger venom housed and pumping into my flesh filling spattering
painting my insides with three searing spurts

                         and your stubble plugs the cries of my mouth as we
             slump together
                         abs convulse and slow and spooning
                         collapsing back into flesh
         i feel you soften slow slipping spent from the broken gasket of my
         hole abused and ruined

                    and from me flows water, mixed with blood

and dented like a can
waiting for your roommate to finish with the shower
i sat in the hall and stank

juan de la cruz
from the spanish

oh flame of living love
that tenderly wounds
my soul's core
no longer shy
finish then, inside me and
rend the veil apart

     oh sweet soreness!
     oh gentle scar!
     oh soft caress!

that knows eternal life
and knows each pain
and pays each debt
and trades for me a dying death

oh lamp of fire
in whose resplendence
the dark blind cavern illumines
and with strange beauties
casts warmth and light
upon your beloved

and with love and gentleness
you stir in me secretly
and the scent of your breath
glorious and good
swells my heart with love

to reproach mystics with
loving God by means of the faculty
of sexual love is as though one were
to reproach a painter with making
pictures by means of colours
composed of material substances

we haven't anything else with
which to love

—simone weil

as they walked they passed a man who was blind from birth
and they asked him:

> who has sinned
> that this man should be born blind:
> > himself, or his parents?

and he answered:

> neither
> that's really not how this works

and he gave him sight

but it was the sabbath
and some said it was a different man
and they also said: a sinner cannot cure the blind

> but the blind man could see
> all the same

and one day we walked past the stall of a tax collector named matthew.
you looked at him counting his coins and he was struck terrified when he
saw you like a bear had fallen upon him from the hills and you said

    follow me

and he got up from his booth and left
spilling coins into the mud and trampling them there as he hustled in
your wake

and that night while we ate at matthew's house among its beautiful
furnishings and delicious fare the traitor complained bitterly that we
ought not to delight in such fine things or move with such corrupt people
and you said

    i came to save the sick
        not the well
    to heal the poisoned
        not the hearty
    to call the sinner
        not the righteous

    the filth of the alleys and the ditches is as nothing to
    the filth of the stock markets and the boardrooms

we will give salvation not sanctimony
    or we'll never get anywhere

and from the earth i saw another beast rise
        with two horns like a lamb
        and whose voice was the dragon

        and it deceived all the world to worship the first beast
                with his words and his signs

                and they raised a great idol to the beast
                and caused it to live
                        and speak
                and devour all who would not worship

        and the beast causeth all
                great and small, rich and poor, free and captive
                to receive its mark

                that none should buy nor sell without it

let him that hath understanding count the number of the beast
                for it is the number of a man

                and it is 666

parchment comes from *parchemin*
and it was by the road you left me
i am the text you left behind

> behold: the pergamum altar is captive to new empires
> on its frieze the gods in aspic
> olympians hack-limb and blind
> wrestle the giants

>> and
>> they will lose
>> for in youthful ardour the new-fledged pantheon mistook
>> sunkissed battle for a war of ageless date
>> tricked into the rock

> and there in encroaching ruin the titans thrive
> shrieking kids of chaos and old night gibbering writhe
>> eating art and stone

> now evicted divinity cockroaches into the utter dark
> and an island of ruins clogs the river spree
> to teach thee:
>> how by centuries and by inches
>> a god can die

> and somewhere crushed in the rubble the peeled wreckage of a faun
> flayed in ecstasy blister burnt
> remembering a blade in your teeth your foot on my chest
>> as your thumb unseamed my skin

> time wins there isn't time
write on the paper of pergamum
and to the church that is in pergamum write

par chemin by the road from emptied cereus-bloom gethsemane after
wriggling from the pig policemen's grasp and my own best jacket i found
a tattered canvas dropcloth
a rag to cover myself a dignity i do not need except as expedience except to
rummage catastrophe and pluck back my heart
and i groped my way in the city dark towards the door of the high
priest's house

where peter is already begging at the grate
i watch the face of the woman at annas's gate soften then twist again into
perplexity

      that i who am client-son to the leper councillor should fall to so
      mean a state
naked and ragged, desperate

      there is a time when the operation of the machine becomes so
      odious makes you so sick at heart that you can't take part you
      can't even passively take part and you've got to put your bodies
      upon the gears and upon the wheels and upon the levers upon
      all the apparatus and you've got to make it stop and you've
      got to indicate to the people who run it to the people who own
      it that unless you're free the machine will be prevented from
      working at all

      and knowing i am hopeless she raises the portcullis with pity
      and lets us in

peter's accent she clocks directly and they launch their firelit interrogations
but i cannot care
i push past the huddle and the black and grope for

                          where are you going?

a guard. he is not one of the city officers but a roman soldier. part of a
detachment lent to the high priest for the festivities waiting to escort you
haunting the forecourt lest they desanctify the house with their stink

                        who are you looking for?

      please. they have taken away my master
      and i do not know where they have laid him

      please
      tell me where he is

i realize i am crying shivering dirty hysterical only after he does and he is
gentle and kind and pulls me to himself. he is not the soldier whose
beloved you had healed but he might as well be handsome and athletic
thick brows and thick eyelashes and smelling of the barracks

> oh. you're one of them
> the arrest tonight
> i'm sorry

saint sebastian was a roman soldier. hot idiot twink go-go dancer pass-around
party bottom of the lord pincushioned through with arrows
> a sagittation it is called: to be pierced by a thousand shafts
> how wonderful how noble to die beautifully for god
> and be done

> [but he didn't die the boy. he survives the arrows and lives covered
> forever in the sores of his devotion
> > for this he is patron saint of plagues
> > a broken apollo infected whole and holy
>
> > saint sebastian pray for us]

> geez
> come here

and i wonder as he holds me as he presses warm metal breastplate against
the shiver: have they already arraigned you? are you encircled envultured
among the sober second thought of the council or are they done their joke
and if so are you somewhere in the dark windows are you watching this
man touch me in the dark one hand atop the scratching burlap but one
significantly already finding its way under my arm onto my bare back

this small mercy simple kindness

which is a very silly thing to wonder, considering. deeds done in darkness
come crashing to the light and there is no shadow you have afforded me
nowhere i can suck annihilation. foxes have dens and birds their nests but
the children of men have no place to lay their heads

saint sebastian became a soldier to "help the martyrs"
which is a nice way of saying he was a collaborator
who spared a soul now and then
who made it quick
who made it so it didn't hurt
who let the family have the body

but the soldier is sweet and his
voice is soft and easy

and i spit in his face

Cerinthus! whom i have abjured
to whom i have been unkind
        whose bones by now are powder
        clean and fine

have you seen the magdalene's head
        Cerinthus
how the french bottled her blackened skull like a perfume
like some cosmonaut visiting from a universe of death
        grinning rictus from inside the skittering brass martian helm
        nothing looks less like grace to me

once i turned a corner in amboise
and underfoot crushed roses wrapped like corpses in plastic
and in confusion saw
i had put my sneaker flat upon the neat flat top of da vinci
        who died in exile
        wailing that he had wasted his talents
                who cursed the youth salaì
                for distracting him with his beauty
                for squandering his hours with muddy dalliance
                and in pay inherited la giaconda for quick resale
        after the revolution when the peasants sacked the pleasant loire
        they found the old master's brainpan tossed in the garden
                cracked
                his big head filled with soil
        (smelt alexander so? *pah!*)

    in any case
    they have a wrought iron railing there now
        because of me

maybe you had it right Cerinthus
        maybe the meat was the problem

you left nothing behind
        not a word
        not a token
        and your cologne that i complained of
                        i never nosed again

i hope your end was kind Cerinthus
i hope your god was too

kinder than i was, and
        kinder than mine was to me

i took her to mass once
because i wanted to be nice
      and it was nice but
then the homily from the tepid insipid pastor
took a sudden sideswipe about the sanctity of the family
praying to restore the natural order
      and i felt my face get hot and
      all my skull's gaskets steam and fire and
      i said i'd wait outside

when she came out balancing with
her walker and saw i had been crying she
said:

              don't make me choose
              between you and my god

              because you will lose

cold as stone

and i felt something important
crack

      but i suppose
      i made the same choice
      didn't i

you spat blood onto the cold white marble tile

your back is a torn mass scabbed to the rough rag naked

        they have twisted a cruel gnarl of thorns around your head
    and i cannot bear the sight of it

        wraith and wreath and writhe and wrath all come from the
    same root they are all a shape twisting around a hollowness they are
    all defined by the spiralizing loss of a centre

        when is a pound of flesh like a ring?

on his dais the governor barely looks up from his agenda at the dissident
insurgent on his floor

    well here is the man
    here is your king

and from the crowd all around me a howl caught between the heel of
caesar and the chant of the mob. yes a king and more my whole life i have
left peter crying in the high priest's forecourt at his own denials but i do
not have time for weakness i do not have time for coddling i do not care
about integrity i am the son of the thunder i would deny everything pull
my limbs from their sockets sell every piece of me i need only jostle and
wrench you from this the shaft of rock around which only i am and the
white-sheeted roman asks: are you? king?

and from somewhere in the rag pile of tatters shitting blood comes your voice
not in whirlwind not in earthquake not in fire but still and small and clear

    i am whatever you say i am
    i don't care about that

    to this end i was born and
    for this only i am in the world:

        to bear witness to the truth

and at this, finally, the roman, whose casual occupation has crushed our
suborned homeland under his regime's foot
looks up with an urbane sneer, amused intrigued and i sink. he hands his
paperwork to a deferential aide, and leans towards the ruin deposited
before him. with him swells the attracted gaze of something terrible and
immortal that has been looking for you since the wilderness

and the prefect vicious and officious asks:
truth? what is truth?

        and i knew
        the cross was inevitable after that

if all you said was thank you
that would be enough

the eye through which i see and
the eye through which god sees me are
the same eye

we are all the mothers of god
for god seeks always to be born

theologians quarrel
mystics concur

love is
       stronger than death
       harder than hell
death only cleaves soul from body
       but
love cleaves all away entire

but if you seek the kernel
you must break the shell

                —meister eckhart

the sun was sunk

we had put you in the earth—the borrowed tomb of some rich man you
had impressed—and i filled my eyes for the last time with the broken,
folded sight of your body grown cold. shrunken somehow, the skin
tightened and whitened where it had not been split like the peel of a
dropped plum across the kitchen tile

they pulled it from your mother's wailing arms and wrapped it in
bandages and tucked it away. it did not look like you, and i wish i had
never seen it

i shuffled back alone in the dusk. the holiday had already begun and every
door was shut up snug and i walked between the city rising behind and
the dormer town of bethany in front, its windows glowing in the gloam.
an expanse dead and desolate. stripped clean, as though to even speak
would summon language that had no place amid a silence from before the
foundations of the earth were laid

then i saw it

standing beside the road the wizened, rotten husk. a spike splintered and
blackened like a lightning strike like a dead twisted match. the fig tree you
had cursed

you had been hungry, irrational, swearing, embarrassing. it was not the
season for figs. you had no right. the earth has rules and timetables and to
everything there is a season and it was not fair. to ask so much from
something so bright, and green, and innocent

> and i knew then what you must have known: that you would never
> see another season of figs

> i reached into the turncoat's pocket whose clothes i still wore and
fished from it a flash of silver. some of the prize that cost us everything
cold and clean. and i saw

and kneeling in the dust with a jagged coin that cut my hand i carved our
names, yours and mine, into the mottled bark

and i looked at the coin, the imperial face impressed ineptly upon it. give
unto the emperor what is the emperor's give unto god what is god's
and what then is left for me. squatting before another graven image.
carving scars to worship. i flung the ugly thing into the dirt

and then my back against the broken trunk beneath its dead and drying
branches by the river kidron i sat down and wept

and when the lamb had opened the seventh seal
    heaven fell silent

and an angel came forth before the altar that is before the throne
    and in his hands he swung a censer
    from which poured as smoke the prayers of the saints

and then the angel filled the censer with the altar's fire
    and cast it from the verge of heaven
    over its crystal battlements

        and in voices and lightning
        and thunder and quake

        it smote into ruin the face of the earth

from my house at patmos
from my porch swing creaking
from atop the ziggurat of the babel spire
i see a serpent blot out a third of the stars
  belched hot from ruined hell and dragging in his wake
  the flotsam debris of a universe of death
      eye of jet nictitating bent fast upon our world

there suspended glittering upon its golden chain will he coil and gnaw
revenge into the root-rotten earth
  till it tatters in his teeth tears and with the setting sun will tumble
  skittering splintered shivers like a shattered chandelier

and as the light from our floating flensing world flecks skin scaling and
seeping i wonder: how it feels against his scars
    he and i know what it is to outlive our grace. he and i
    have slithered over stone in a crackled wilderness
    parched and seasonless

our maker made monsters of us both. of the deep and heights and wastes
tore the thing we loved to scraps and dared us leering to cry out

so i watch the Great Serpent who is called Satan make planetfall and drop
to crawl through the underbrush and hot dirt
  a brand of fire in his tail
  sidewinding through a landscape of kindling
  red rust rim rising across the meadows and mounting to melt the world

let them raise high the maypole Nehushtan. let come every hour and every man
let enmity breed between their seething seed:
  to bruise heads and heels alike
  till all the graves stand tenantless, yawning to yield up their sleepers
    while the sheeted dead squeak and gibber in the streets

still i will remember you. on a spraying beach in the damp
still i will remember the funk the wet the hair the touch the heat the scruff
the mouth the taste the glow the kiss the stomach the spit the breath
  i will remember. and thy commandment all alone shall live
  within the book and volume of my brain

dragons live forever, but not so little boys
let me be a dragon then
let the waters sour
take my milk for gall
       and from my dug let all the earth
       be poisoned with its wormwood

before i was created i am where i was

there are neither angels nor saints
        nor this
        nor that

many speak of the eight heavens
        of the nine choirs

        they are not where i am

        all these statements
        all these images
        all these faiths

they but point the way

        in god is nothing but god

        and no soul comes to god
        until it becomes god

        no one comes to the naked god
        until they are themselves naked

        and dancing on the head of a pin
        must be nothingness itself

                        —catherine treatise
                        translated from the middle high german

what you seek
is seeking you

apocalypse proliferates. as lies multiply, apocalypse promises meaning, however dreadful. the yearning for armageddon is a desire to instantiate certainty in moments of disorder. its unveiling (that is all the word means) assures that something worth the veiling is behind the curtain: a sense of an ending—the naked lunch, when we at last will see what is on the end of every fork

these crises, in which it becomes impossible to imagine any truth or
meaning to history, can then be understood as a recurrent
phenomenon, as a part of the unfolding of history itself, when the
yokes of tyrannies and empires and capital become at once too
much to bear yet impossible to imagine ending

there came a moment, living both under a conquering empire and as an unwelcome new sect in a culture struggling to survive the destruction of its capital site, when they realized you weren't coming back as soon as they hoped. in growing numbers but dwindling faith, they saw that those who were waiting for the blessed day were growing old, were dying
                                        where was the promised end

when they speak of a terrible final horror or dreadful cataclysm, when i
    see for myself the sky crack and the sea boil, i think of you: dirty and
        sweet, gleaning for food in the field like a sparrow, taking water in
gulping greedy mouthfuls from whoever would give it in half-labelless
        plastic water bottles of unknown provenance, resigned to cheerful
    powerlessness among the casualties and collateral damage of empires
            and kings: fishermen, potters, shepherds, housewives, whores

someday you saw a day when the world will turn upside down, when last are first and widow and orphan are comforted, but you seemed spectacularly bored by the timelines and details

                        you shall not say of the kingdom of god:
                        here it is or there it is

                it is here
                now
                among you

now i wait in that yawning space you left me in
watching empires shed like magnolia petals on the loam

listening for tumblers in the lock of history to click

we are the vine
you and i
    continuous
    connected
    cultivated

we are the stem of a seed long planted
we are the fruit the hungry world awaits

put forth a branch

a question comes from a space that does not even know how to ask for
what it wants, that barely finds the breath to hope for hope:

lord teach us how to pray

i think they wanted something incantatory and magisterial; some runic
baroque utterance that would spin open all the airlocks and gaskets. an
omnipotent and omniscient divine does not need us to vocalize the
anxieties that plague us or the wishes that consume us but i suppose
sometimes we do

do not pray too much
        too long and too loud
        asking to grant queries
        to which you yourselves are supposed to be the answer

                there is enough if you
                share it

and when you must pray, say only this:

and you gave them a peasant's mantra:

not just king but father
not just them but us
        a kingdom always coming
        and a trial we would be spared

someday the just will get their rewards
someday the world will split apart

worrying about it is not ours to do, and
not even the Son knows the hour
        tomorrow will come
        the end will come
                revolution is not an event
                it is a work we are working
                like yeast into dough

just give us the bread we need today
and help us forgive others and ourselves for yesterday

        that's all

you get off the train with your ratty little red backpack and i leap from james's car and race to you and kiss you in front of the groaning hydraulics. the holidays with my family. you do not seem excited but who could blame you

at home my father is his usual brusque thundercloud but you manage this as you always do. every conversation seems the conversation you were born to have and if he says anything racist i don't hear him

later at my aunt's house there is the tumult of my cousins and the smell of frying things and the endless piles of seafood and whenever i look at you your lips are red from pepper sauce and red wine (how much wine have you had?) and your plate is heaped again. i catch you outside and you say you needed air and it is true the house is sweating with the sheen of hot sweaters and screaming child athletics and you squeeze my hand

that night after midnight presents (i got you a new backpack, you forgot me but it is your birthday after all it's fine) in my childhood bed that feels entirely too small for you, like a wizard in a hobbit hole you lie with your feet sticking over the bed's edge and you say

    i only ever make you sad

come live with me and be my love and we shall all these pleasures prove and then you pull me roughly drunkenly inexpertly atop you and after a few incomplete jabs and whines of the bed frame you cum, thick and startling in gobs and you fall haphazardly into a noisy snore that harmonizes with my father's down the hall

                      and i find a way to perplexing sleep

the next day we meet your mother at the train to join us and she is so excited to see me i feel a strange selfish pride as though in catching her i have caught the part of you that i cannot catch my intercessor my most gracious advocate

at dinner with your glass full again your mother says to mine that we are lucky to have found each other and i beam at you but you seem not to have heard. and then my mother, who hates this who loves me and hates what i am and what the world knows that i am, asks in a half joke that turns my father's stomach

so when will you make it official
when will my son sit at your right hand

and you look up from your pile of shrimp confused and you say

    never?

like glass stuck into my neck

later i find you dozing away your wine in the sitting room, near the
tinselled tree, under the heap of my cousins' uncountable children's coats
whose sticky owners are wrestling in the basement
to wayward winter reckoning yields
and i sink next to the couch and lean against you and your hand finds my
hair. i watch the ornaments of plastic and glass that my family has
amassed over a lifetime turning gently in the LED glow

    it's never going to be the happy ending you want
    you know that

        and i do

        and i kiss your fingers, and find the plastic cup of your wine on
the hardwood, and take a sip

        and watch the lights twinkle in the plastic tree
        and the glass eyes of its angel surveying

        a storm that is blowing in from paradise

in edinburgh go down to the bottom of the street, careening out of the
castle and past the statue of rob the bruce, past the end of the world, and
past holyrood house where david rizzio hid in the skirts of the queen of
scots's dress before they disgorged the little italian faggot like a haggis

and you will find the ruins of an abbey—soaring gothic windows
glassless, stonework overgrown with mosses and apostasy

all its royal tombs desecrated
its vaults collapsed into a roofless ruin

open to the sky

when first you practise contemplation
you will experience only a darkness
a cloud of unknowing

you will not know what it is
you will only know that in your heart you feel a simple longing
a reaching out to God

you must also know that this darkness
this cloud
will forever be between you and your God
whatever you do

it will always blind you
always keep you from understanding
always keep you from fully feeling him
in the sweetness of love

and so
you must make your home
in the darkness

—the cloud of unknowing

i write to you elect lady
i write to you gaius
            i commend to you demetrius
            and
            i warn against diotrephes

            who will not acknowledge us
listing
under the mass times
            which parts of us
            we can keep
and seeping a fear
            still festering

            that any faith would have us
            is a faith too false to hold

      this god is too small
      this the sin against the holy spirit

no. instead
let us love one another
            not in word or speech
            but in truth and action

                  know this, little children:
                  if
                        in our guilt and sorrow and loneliness
                        even our own broken hearts condemn us
                        god will not

                  for god is greater than our hearts

comfort the suffering
trouble the powerful
      let all you say be a promise
      let all you say be a threat
and they will hear it as they hear it
from how high up they listen

two by two he sent them
to preach and cast out demons
taking nothing on their journey but a staff
      no bread
      no bag
      no money in their belts

when you enter a town
stay in one house till you leave

      and if the town reject you
      shake the dust from your sandals
      as a testimony against them

my brother he paired with matthias. james would think this a rebuke i
knew but maybe he just thought i needed more time to mend. but as he
sent them off, paired to make a fugitive ark of the world, i felt something
rising like sap to leak from the ligaments of my spine. and when they were
all gone i stood on magdala's beach and asked in a voice that felt too high:

      and where are *we* going?

      you are going to bethany with mary and martha
      to their father simeon's house
      you are going to heal
      you are going to survive

and he touched my shoulder—kindly, but also to remind me of my arm,
patronizing, disgusting as the tears rose stinging hot in my eyes and i
began to plead

      you could come
      you could forget about all this and be with me

and what shall i say?
"father, save me from this hour"?
but for this i came to this hour

you can't just throw me away
if it's bad i should be with you

they also serve who stand and wait

and i asked the stupid petty question
is there someone
do you want to be with someone else

there is everyone
i had not thought death had undone so many
please
let me spare you the cup i'll drink

and i felt the floor drop—no not quite that i felt the atoms of the world slip apart and degauss and i fell through them unsynced defragmented, tumbling like through a world of particle dust. like the letter case of a print shop had tumbled out and spilled all its alphabets across the workman's floor

i swallowed the torrent i felt rising because i was not sure if it was words or vomit
and i turned, and ran up the strand

and the footprints on the beach were all my fucking own

in the cellar smokes the prophet
        mottled moonlit stump incensing to heaven
        hairy carcass still handsome in its wreckage
        pooling cold stone onyx in the craggle of the light

while on her damasked divan the princess twisted
        giddy at the gift of approaching platter dish
        whisking silvered dome with a pretty flourish
        falling rapt with tears upon his bloodied bloodless lips

i too have loved a madman
        who chose his holiness and not me
        i too have ached for prophet-flesh
        like a carrion bird pinwheeling in the upper air

        i too have wept washed fondling all my cradled ruin
        i too have tasted blood, kissing all my world
        goodbye

hadewijch of antwerp
from the brabantian middle dutch

all
is too small
to hold me
i am too vast

from infinity
i reach
for uncreated

i touch it
it undoes me
wider than wide

all else is
too narrow

you know this well
for you are also there

at Pentecost the firebird fell
the fire fell as tongues of flame
in the form of fire the spirit fell
and me it ravished

banging shrieking screaming
in blazing burning starsong

      once around the grass
      and twice around the lass
      and thrice around the maple tree

i smelt the sugars of my mind caramelize and boil
every cell bursting incandescent
a scroll on my tongue a coal on my lips a hot iron thrust in my fundament

    i shall be your gaveston your ganymede

    i will speak in a thousand tongues, in a thousand voices will i speak,
with no fetter or chain to bind me
    burst like an old wineskin flush with new

    fuck me in the dirt of the street make me your darling
    and i will serve you naked

      let there be no longer any secret what you do to me
      spurting hot across my face as i lick you foaming clean
      before the throngs and choirs of angels
      your bitch your bottom
filling your toxic cup in heaven before the celestial court in just a
spotting soaking thong

      then let them press their wet cloacas to me ravaged by eagle
talons tearing engorged rend me apart and then

let me be in a thousand ruined fragments shored
let the wind buffet and blow me where it will
      your ragdoll sexdoll sweetheart

let the broad icicle of you plunge like a stalactite dagger in my heart and
frost and melt and run across the edges of the flat-struck rotundity of the
world and sprinkle cool water on the souls who burn across the chasm

      do you have poison for me? i will drink it
      unsex me and index me here old break-back moloch
      prime of belphegor, maxwell's fussing spirit

let the legion of gadarene make me its whore if only you will watch and
praise me after

      for you i will be their common trough
      boil me in all the oil of every vat in rome
      and receive their piss streaming against my tonsils in the urinal of
      my mouth
      let my body testify that i have sung your praises while they took me
      and broke me on their wheel and forced their fists groaning inside me
      babbling in the twisting muscular tongues of men till they tore the
      instrument from my throat
            let me be soaked in the cum of nations
            pure and debased utterly for love of you

then when it is done and i am whimpering in the hot shiver of the blood
and semen that coats me as a crust as a slime

      please wash me

      your virgin slut
      my master my sir
      tell me that i have done well, your good and faithful servant
      lick me clean like a mother bear her cub

      and let me at last be rested
      black fire on white fire
      silent and forgiven in the crook of your arm

behold then: the victim
in that state which the Spirit
     (loving them infinitely
     in the purity of their soul)

     reduces them

      painful
      fixed and bound

     so He can bring them to a condition
     where He wishes to take His pleasure in them

the bed is narrow
but you must make room
     so that He will be its only Master
     its only Spouse
     and its free and gentle Owner

          —marie de l'incarnation

be the light
    however vast the dark

fish cannot drown in water
birds do not fall from the sky
and in the fire of the forge
gold is not extinguished

      but rather
      the fire brightens

if each thing god made
lives in its own truth
how could i resist my own nature
the thing that i was made for
      how could i not
      burn in oneness with god?

    —mechthild of magdeburg

master how often should i forgive my brother?
       as many as seven times?

              should?
              you should never forgive anyone
              it wouldn't mean anything
                   if you should do it

                   but instead

              forgive carelessly
                   imprudently
                   thoughtlessly
                   let them make a fool of you

              let all the world laugh
                   as you are gulled and conned
                   and cucked

              forgive them
              not seven times
                   but seven times seventy

in the gardens of the leper i dozed in the afternoon sun. mary was in the markets of bethany, and martha was in the kitchen as she always was, perfecting a pie or her scowl

their father simeon was a judicious but generous man with a pale blotch upon his scalp and face. we had played one game of chess, during which he asked me absolutely no questions about my life or person and which i very carefully lost, and it seemed i had met with some measure of his satisfaction, after which i became one of the various objects cluttering up his house along with mary's seashells or martha's glittering copper pots. i accompanied the family on their various social ablutions to sanhedrin dinners and festivals and rumour spread that i was the leper's son returned which made mary snort

he usually returned late from the temple complex, where the priests and officials made their last countdown preparations for the city to swell with pilgrims and soldiers for the festival. we thus had the run of the house, which martha largely managed and mary largely upended, while i tried to strike the politest balance of both, like their desperate eager terrier

i had as the weeks slipped by become martha's primary sampler, and she watched me try every tart or roasted bird with sober, patient contempt at my peasant palate and ignorant suggestions while i felt my middle pleasantly slightly soften, spared the road's dehydrations and exertions. and your exertions

she was doing her best with me, in her way

mary did her best in her way too—sad movies and minted face masks and loud excoriations of all your million beauties and kindnesses. she introduced me to hopeless shy closet-cases at parties and gave me too much to drink and when i ended up just crying and saying something nice about you she would pinch me, hard, at the elbow or love handle

they were both good sisters to me

    but i was lost. just stacking days

batter my heart three-person'd god, for you
as yet but knock, breathe, shine, and seek to mend;
that i may rise and stand, o'erthrow me, and bend
your force to break, blow, burn, and make me new

i like an usurp'd town to another due
labour to admit you—but o, to no end.
reason, your viceroy in me, me should defend,
but is captived and proves weak or untrue

yet dearly i love you and would be loved fain
but am betroth'd unto your enemy;
divorce me, untie or break that knot again
take me to you. imprison me, for i

>   except you enthrall me never shall be free
>   nor ever chaste, except you ravish me

—donne, holy sonnet XIV

i lay in bed at the close of day and had barely closed my eyes
when a figure in the shape and form of a man, his face hidden,
came down from above and lay atop me. his weight sank down
on me, and he filled the whole substance of my soul, pressing
into me in a way that i can't put into words, and i took him in
faster and deeper than the softest wax is able to receive the
strongest impressed seal

this shook me suddenly from the dream, and now awake i still
felt a sweet weight inside me, and i was delighted, and what shall
i say? my soul melted, my soul, lord, almost broke loose, almost
poured out of my body

indeed, if i am honest, if that sudden overflowing gush of holy
pleasure had continued much longer, it would have by its very
strength drawn the soul swiftly from my body like a torrent, like
a wave, and bore it away, had it not ebbed away, little by little

from then on, however, my mouth has been open, and i have not
been able to stop writing. even now, even if i wanted to, i could
not be silent

and hanging above the altar i beheld him, living, in my mind's
eye. i took hold of him, him whom my soul loves. i held him. i
embraced him. i kissed him lingeringly, and feeling how
gratefully he accepted this gesture of my love, between my kisses
he himself opened his mouth, so that i could kiss him all the
more deeply

—rupert of deutz

the smell of your hand clamped earthy over my mouth from behind me
        on the floor my pants ruck down my ass pale my dick hard and
caught and useless in my still-fastened jeans

your hips fit snug to me bucking rutting breeding fucking me huffing
hot bull's ox breath behind my ear
then i feel the stretch and quiver grunt and guttural and
        your ridge wide inflamed forces past the tight ring and closes there
like a wound, locked inside like the head of a knot
        like the piece of the fruit adam swallowed lodged forever in his throat

and you stop, and rear up above me, surveying the span of my back, and with
my face in the ancient carpet stains you whisper like they are the first words

        fuck i love you

and pull me up to kiss you backwards like a beast of myth like some
terrible atomic monster fused bruised flesh of adam perichoresis
coinherence the fur of your stomach mopping the sweat of my back
hand upon my hummingbird throat and while the heavy muscle of your
tongue twists inside my mouth

                        and i realize—i accept—that he is me and i am you
                                only he is more of me than i am

i feel your pulse thrum through the thickened, thickening vein of you
inside the base of me

        every inch a king

i should have been smashed apart
    drowned like a hylas
    teeth and face broken and cracked like a hyacinth
    fucked to death like troilus against an altar plinth
        my brains dashed out and leaking

    i deserved that mercy

a god should at least clean up after himself
pick up and rinse his battered toys
toss the crumpled cum-rag in the hamper
close the tab and spare the souls trapped there their deathless labours

    instead i persisted

and sleeping in the orchard—my custom always of the afternoon—i watched
an adder fearless and unfeared sidewind across the grass, well stored with
subtle wiles

and i saw it move in tract oblique, curling wanton wreaths, and i saw what
intelligence shimmered in its carbuncled eye, subtlest beast of the field

and i wondered if i should cry out
and i did not cry out

    and upon my heel it fastened
        and blossomed there a bruise

                sharp teeth the knot of me intrinsicated and
              swift as quicksilver its malice coursed through
                    all the gates and alleys of my veins
                    posseting and curdling all my blood
            filling my mind with desperate clicking scorpions
                    and i whimpered on the grass
            smiling smelling at the end your breath like hay

    and then i knew the joy of the worm
    a dark not black but red

all hail the carrion king

and the body you had loved and threw away
was encrusted, tettered, barked about

      in a vile and loathsome lazar

the sisters sent word from bethany saying, the one you love is
sick. and he hesitated to come so close to jerusalem again, but
then he said:

we must go back
south to judea

but, his disciples said, a short while ago they tried to
stone you there, and will surely kill you if you return,
and yet you are going back there?

and he answered angrily:

are there not twelve hours of daylight?
a man who walks by day will not stumble
for he sees by this world's light

it is when he walks by night that he
stumbles
for he has no light

after he had said this, he went on to tell
them:

he has fallen asleep only
but i am going there
to wake him up

his disciples replied, if he sleeps, he will
get better

so then he told them plainly:

he is dead, he is slain on the heights
and you and this wretched world are
lucky i was not there

but let us go to him

then thomas (called didymus), who
saw the danger, said to the rest of the
disciples, let us also go, that we may
all die together

on his arrival in bethany, he found that his
beloved disciple had already been in the
tomb for four days

and many had come to the sisters to comfort
them in their loss of their brother. and the
disciples were nervous to be only a few miles
from jerusalem. but he did not care. when
martha heard that he was coming, she went
out to meet him, but her sister mary refused.
and martha accused him, saying:

if you had been here, he would not
have died
but i know that even now god will give
you whatever you ask

and he said to her:

he will rise again

and she answered, i know he will rise
again in the resurrection at
the last day

and he said to her:

no. now

i am who am the resurrection and
the life

who believes in me will live, even
though he die

and whoever lives and believes in
me will never die

and after she had said this, she went
back and called her sister: the teacher is
here, she said, and is asking for you

when mary heard
this, she got up and
went to him

when those who had been with
mary in the house, the rich and
powerful friends of her father
from the temple precincts,
comforting and paying their
respects to their family, noticed
her rush to get up and go out,
they so followed her, supposing
she was going to the tomb to
mourn there

and when mary and the crowd who followed
her reached the place where he was and saw
him, she fell at his feet weeping, demanding:

if you had been here
he would not have
died

where have you laid him?
he asked. come and see
she replied. and she showed
him the tomb

and he wept

and those who saw him weeping
said, see how he loved him!

but some said, could not he who worked
miracles have kept this man from dying?

once again deeply moved, he came to the
tomb. it was a cave with a stone laid
across the entrance

take away the stone

it has been four days
said martha. he will
stink

move the stone. see
the glory of god

so they took away
the stone. and he
cried out:

come out!

clement of alexandria
mar saba fragment

[and they come into bethany. and a
certain woman whose brother had died
was there. and, coming, she prostrated
herself before him and says to him, son
of david, have mercy on me. but the
disciples rebuked her

but he, being angered, went off with
her into the garden where the tomb
was, and straightway a great cry was
heard from the tomb. and going near
he rolled away the stone from the
door of the tomb. and straightway,
going in where the youth was, he
stretched forth his hand and raised
him, seizing his hand

but the youth, looking upon him, loved
him and began to beseech him that he
might be with him

and going out of the tomb they came
into the wealthy house where stayed the
youth. and after six days he told him
what to do and in the evening the youth
comes to him, wearing a linen cloth over
his naked body

and he remained with him that night,
and he taught him the mystery of the
kingdom of God

and thence, arising, he returned to the
other side of the jordan where]

there's a moment

    i'm forgetting
    that i forgot
    that i

i feel my eyes unstitch and cotton clogging my mouth my sinuses full of
clots and cough and gasp and spit the nodules and the wadded mass
from my throat. bandages strips of cloth tear away like spiderwebs it is
dark and my skin is scaled and lazarous and the crust pulls with the linen
dark dark all dark

no. light

this is my grave

i sit up and i am covered in the putrescence of the serpent's sores but it
sloughs from me in sheets, lazar cracking like an old scab like a cicada
nymph like a lobster pulling from its husk and underneath tithonus
mucus exuvia i am soft and i am vital i am clean and

i stand, and totter towards the thin crescent of dusty dusking light

in the bright of the olive grove mary is weeping in the dirt and a crowd
massive and important and stricken stares at me in my nakedness except
for the last strips on my hands and feet and

     it's you

and you touch her shoulder as my eyes adjust to the light

     woman why do you weep

     for this thy brother was dead
     and is alive again

     was lost
     and is found

and you fall on my neck
and kiss me with the kisses of your mouth

when lazarus left his charnel-cave
    and home to mary's house returned
    was this demanded: if he yearned
to hear her weeping by his grave?

"where wert thou brother, those four days?"
    there lives no record of reply
    which telling what it is to die
had surely added praise to praise

from every house the neighbours met
    the streets were filled with joyful sound
    a solemn gladness even crowned
the purple brows of olivet

behold a man raised up by christ!
    the rest remaineth unrevealed
    he told it not, or something sealed
the lips of that evangelist

                    —tennyson

you washed me and cleaned me from the dust and slime of the grave and dressed me in white terrycloth and now i recline against your chest, my head reeling faint, feeling you hard as stone behind me

i let the sinews of my neck droop into you and you cup my forehead and whisper against me

and your hand is roving

     really

    turn me on dead man

    be gentle buddy i'm still broken

    never. never broken
    and never gentle

and you open my robe and i flop there stiffening, slightly ridiculous and swelling in a proud, embarrassed crest. whoa see there you are. not so broken after all as you draw your finger carefully over the oozing slit at the top of me and pull away a tacky translucent strand definitely another amazing miracle by me, miracle guy

and you kiss the sole of each foot as you raise them by the ankle, and sink the curls of your head between my parting lap

and my joy is as a sword

the rooms of the leper's mansion are full and loud and happy. news of what you have done—the lost soul you have delivered from perdition—has spread everywhere, and simeon is throwing you a party in which i am at once guest of honour and celebrated adoptee and sideshow freak

your followers flood south from all the eddies of their missions to congregate here. my brother and peter and andrew arrive together and hug me much too tight and my brother i think manages not to cry. james's travelling companion matthias whom i barely know shakes my hand and offers some polite, absurd congratulations and in his defence i am not sure what to say either

people look at me like an oddity, surprised that i am hale, trying to see if they can catch any flickers of the grave behind my eyes. like i might start feasting for brains. what was it like? i can do nothing but disappoint them

i see the zealot and the traitor in a corner in animated conversation and when he notices me the traitor offers a smile that twitches into a sneer. they know this has decided things finally. tomorrow you will march against jerusalem and either the walls will fall or we will be dashed apart like a storm's wave against them. along with me an engine that is now unstoppable has sputtered to life. from the cliff face at masada the zealot's hopes will tear themselves on the rocks, but so few of us will live to see even that disappointment

as we recline at dinner martha circulates food while you talk with simeon. he is trying to get you to make some kind of address in the city with witness testimonials, wheeling me out like a prop. i can feel the rumble of a laugh in your chest you do not vocalize, and you give my left butt cheek a quick melon squeeze. there is the game of lamb upon your hot breath

it is then that mary enters. she carries an expensive carafe and bows to you. and with it she anoints your hair and feet as the room falls into hush and the fragrance of nard thick and musky fills the air

simeon twists in mortification at the scene and at mary, who passes when she wishes to but tonight is unadorned, without makeup, in a shapeless garment, her hair snapped in its clip, no perfume but the perfume she puts upon your skin. and somewhere in the room the traitor snarls about the waste of money, but you rebuke him:

        to justify your meanness tomorrow
      even if i won't be
let her do her kindness

i peel away from you to let her work and i recognize the scent from the rags of my tomb and i realize: this is the oil she bought for my funeral. this is the oil she used to anoint my broken body when they put me in my grave

and as i look around the room at friends and strangers balking in horror and contempt at this grand expensive intimacy, i share the thought she has already finished: that they will come for you. that you bought my life with your death

i watch her work out her thanks and her farewell and her fuck-you in patterns on your skin that dance and shimmer fresh in the light, then fade as they seep into your soft and tender flesh

in the dim upper room lit by a few shuddering candles, twelve embarrassed workmen quietly peel off a pile of dirty sock half-wrecked sneaker and muddy sandal

    slapping the pads of our feet against cold tile in halos of condensation

whispering in close-breath giggle, mortified as the sharp reek of corn-chip and beer-sour esters mixes with the warm shimmer of myrrh

    hammertoe and yellow nail, roughened heel and grime

and listening to the gentle splash of milky water in a basin while naked on your knees among a forest of our calves

    warm suds firm hand cotton towel

    fresh and bright and peppermint sting

            you gently rinse us clean

after dinner and the pageant with the bread and wine and the accusations and the acrimony i crept from the humidity of the party and out onto the veranda

in the night air in the garden where i died the softening spring soil is mingling its loam with the acridity of the pollen as the olive trees reach ancient, gnarled branches and white feathering flowers towards the kite of the passover moon. oliveiras can live for millennia half-dreaming witness to ten thousand full moons while they brew bitterness like an alembic. it is the pascal moon the moon of worms when the earth wakes up hungry

      would you rather be forgotten or hatefully remembered

i look for the vulture voice and see the traitor slumped in the porch his sneer lit by the ember of his cigarette. after he had stormed out i thought never to see him again
        congratulations
        would you like to hear what happens next?
        i am a prophet new-inspired

        in the crowd, someone saw—many someones saw
            that you walk again. the cocksucker who was a corpse
      and so these signs and wonders have become too great
            that many now would believe
            that the powderkeg of the city will burst when he touches it
            that the romans will rise like a coiled serpent to strike an
            upstart revolution
            that it is better for one man to die than a whole nation perish

      and from that day since
      because of what he did for your sake
            they now plot to take his life
            and all of us with him

he flicks the spark of the butt into the grove

                  not food, not power, not faith could weaken us
                  it took a little faggot to do it

                  he'll die because he loved you
                  isn't that funny

let them hate me all they want. but you and i know the truth
remember when they kill him
you did it, not me

and he rose
and pushed his tongue past my teeth
his dead hand in my back
his rotten breath filling my mouth

and then he slipped like a loping
scarecrow into the darkness and the trees
where i and the moonlight lost him

                    as   i   have
wandered i have set eyes
upon impregnable Babylon,
on whose walls the chariots
course

                    on Zeus by
          the   banks   of
Alpheus

          on the cascading
gardens,

          on the colossus of
the Sun,

                              on the great
                    man-made   heap   of
                    the   high   glistering
                    pyramids,

                              and the vast
                    tomb-city   of
                    Mausolus

                    but to look
upon the house of the virgin-hunter-
mother

                                        whose eaves scrape the
                    scudding clouds

                    is to see
          these marvels in
          her shadow

                    for the sun
          itself has never
          looked on sight so
          grand

my mouth tastes of smoke
from it i vomited a world of coals

and i lit the coals
that were out of me but not me but
of me
a new thing set burning

i wanted to know if something that
wasn't could be better than that was
i wanted to see a colour that was
new
i wanted to feel you smell
hear you think

i thought if i did it just right and
ordered it just so
eventually there would be you
and it would be perfect

then i just waited
why then and now
it was for you

you are the engine it is for
i knew you before it began and

it does not run without you

in her temple at Ephesus dead Artemis waits dreaming

      gods like people do their best work dead

across marble clicked in place tight and fast by skilful, carcinating hands
like a chessboard my dirty fisherman's sandals shuffle like corrugation

and there she towers:

the multimammia, the Lady of Ephesus, whose statue fell from Jupiter's orbit

      clothed in purple and scarlet
            adorned in gold and jewels and pearls

She, whose high top above the stars did soar,
One foot on Thetis, th' other on the Morning,
One hand on Scythia, th' other on the Moor,
Both heaven and earth in roundness compassing

      bearing her thousand breasts of stone arrayed like artillery
            like ripening cheeses pendant in a cellar

      the goddess who in youth turned Actaeon to a beast for gazing on
her nakedness has now grown shameless—or knows in her fulsome beauty
she has nothing to tempt a catamite like me:

      she can smell another god's musk
            and how deep into the trench of me he has rutted his seed

      only a eunuch emissary then, the devotee of a distant pantheon
            another darting virgin skittering amid the mounting
muffling columns of incense
      curators of the heaps of gold and monstrances and graven images
pirated by the pax romana
      the careful, careless bees who mind her stock portfolio and tend her
glistening honeycomb

and so she meets me with a gaze of placid stone
      dragon atop her treasure hoard, seated on many waters
      with whom the kings of the earth have committed many fornications

and in her hand a cup
    upon whose wine all the world has drunk

       we are survivors, she and i
          midwives to another age

and i stood upon the sand of the sea
and beheld a monster rise
      seven-headed
      ten-horned

and attending it was a beast like a leopard
      foot of bear
      mouth of lion

and one of its heads was dead
      but alive again

      and the authority of the dragon was placed in the beast
      and all the world wondered and worshipped, saying

      who is like the beast?
            and who is able to make war with him?

when last her temple burned artemis the midwife was too
preoccupied with the birth of alexander to stop the rising flame

 now across the basin of the mediterranean the fire is raging again
   my brothers scrambling like foxes with brands in their tails
as samson set upon the fields of the philistines
 and even in the scribbled walls of the precincts of rome alexamenos
is worshipping his donkey-headed god

    the victorious legions who in distant wars
    acquired the vices of strangers and mercenaries
    first oppressed the freedom of the republic and
    afterwards violated the majesty of the purple
    the emperors anxious for their personal safety
    and the public peace were reduced to the base
    expedient of corrupting the discipline which
    rendered them alike formidable to their
    sovereign and to the enemy the vigour of the
    military government was relaxed and finally
    dissolved by the partial institutions of
    constantine and the roman world was
    overwhelmed by a deluge of barbarians

The nymphs in twilight shade of tangled thickets mourn
        with flower-inwoven tresses torn:
Behold what wreak, what ruin, and what waste,
And how that she, which with her mighty power
Tam'd all the world, hath tam'd herself at last,
The prey of time, which all things doth devour

  it has been an age packed like sediment awaiting the dynamite
i am no samson
    but eyeless in gaza i feel my hands upon the temple pillars
    bid to shake this hive of demons upside down

her world was beautiful
let them never say otherwise

i turn
and at the door shake the dust
from off my sandals

        and behind me all the world falls down

Babylon the Great is fallen!

                        she is fallen in her finery

from the high porches of her tower to the pens and stalls of her base court

                     she is trampled by the palace horses

                     she is torn by ranging dogs

                         she is manured in the mud

behold where she lies crumpled

who thought the clockwork of her brain could reverse the course of stars

              gone the gaudy gold, the silver, the stones, the pearls

              gone the linens, the silks, the purples, the scarlet

              gone the ivory, the brass, the iron, the marble

              gone the ointments, the nard, the oil, the wine

her precincts now are the habitations of devils

        her halls the hold of foul spirits

        her ruins the rook of every unclean bird

        cast dust upon your sunken head

        weep in the spaces of her desolation

              see upon the flesh of kings fowls feast amid her streets

Babylon! Bright Babylon!

not a candle in a window more

        shall shine at all in thee

let's ding him down, then he is
done
come sir no need to cry out so
it will not hurt us all this din

gear's all set hammer and where
are the
christ these are fucking savage long
none of that he's scared enough
already
so what let the little traitor piss
himself

lay it flat—oh good grade on this
one
fetched from seed of adam's
mouth they say do they really
well the holes are bored at least
we might have to stretch you a
little
to make the pegs work but

all right time to take that off
will reopen your back a bit i'm
afraid
there's a good lad
s'all right not as bad as that
don't be shy handsome boy like
you fuck
good kirtle though it'll wash i
think but like a
fucking crust on you though phew
never
get that purple out the cambric

he stinks of it already tho to be
honest
for all his fare he shall be flayed

well he's gotta be dead needlings
by noon or we're all in shit
they've got a holiday or something
if it comes to it i brought
the mallet for the femurs anyway
let us haste to hang till he to
death be done

can we take the hat off him at least
better not someone
he claimeth kingdom with a crown
probably has notions about it

poor kid
well he should have watched his
mouth
warlock waxes war than wood
oh fuck off there's no such
i thought he was you know a
terrorist. radicalized
well on the plank go to it
sorry about the back son really
sheesh
this bargain may not blin

all right kid not gonna lie this part
that mark amiss be bored
but it just goes under through the
soft bit
right through here see skids right
through
like hitting the bell at the carnival
and if you hold very still we won't
hit the bone and
there you go there you go
see clean through
good boy good boy shh

nice strong wrists you won't tear
through i don't think
might not even need the rope
sinewy fucker aren't you haha good
buxom the girls must've loved you
ok other side now other side give
me the hand no flinching now
won't be as bad i promise
but listen you can't move because
if we
fuck it up we gotta do it again
and that spot's worse
jeez they could have at least
washed these from the last one two
theeere we go you're safe it's done
little taps clink clink no big deal
you're

fuck it's hot

ok there's a footrest thing down
do you feel that big stretch big
stretch
good just rest them
careful now let's not add
triclavianism to the
there we go right there just rest
them there

now i know the hands were bad
but this is
fuck this is the worst of it
we've gotta go straight through
the foot

pulp the bones up. dancing days
are over i'm afraid
i'm sorry don't cry we'll go quick i
promise jangling like a jay
we're professionals big and strong
aren't we boys
one two

ah fuck he's fucking shat himself
that's all right they all do hey
don't worry about it
nothing to apologize for it happens

ok we're gonna use this cord and
haul you up into that
well i guess you can't see but
there's a whatsit a notch
like a peg in a hole a mortise
tugged to by top and tail lug you up
it'll bounce a little but you're
tight on we did a good job you
won't come asunder
if ye rave ye will not rive
you won't tear off i don't think
and then it's. it's just time
hey. listen it's like going to sleep i
promise
what a brave boy. don't cry
he's so far gone we probably don't
even have to break
shut the fuck up man look at him

lotta people want to see you kid

ready?

we are squatting in one of the leper's upper rooms when mary rushes in. she had gone to your tomb to anoint you after the botch-job of your hasty funeral but i couldn't bear it. not to see you shattered again. but she is crying

he's gone. they have stolen his body

i hear peter wail, his grief and guilt compounded, but i am running. i am not even half-dressed barely a linen cloth gird at my waist and barefoot and the rocks break my feet but i cannot imagine caring. through the streets past the stalls past the lilies of the garden

when i reach the hole they put you in its opening is yawning and inside at the shelf rock where we laid you is nothing but a white shroud. a last desecration. they have fed you to the dogs they have

but then
and then
       i believe

why do you look for the living among the dead?

for a moment i know only instinct shame and i try to cover my nakedness with your shroud but i quake like my knees may break out from under me and i sink to find the stone

and i turn, and look, and you smile, and it is your smile. as i have seen it since we were young, when you found kindness for me when no one else did. help my unbelief

it's you

> i would harrow the field and stone of the world to find you across inches and centuries

> it's only death that's all
> what is that to love

my head swims and i find a strangled stammer i feel the table of the world crack as death works backwards

and you kiss me. and you are warm and soft as i shiver in the creeping dawn of your broken grave

and there among the lilies
i forgot which of us was which
as everything sad became untrue

what are you doing

    what?

where did you even get that hat

      it's a gardening hat! i'm gonna trick the magdalene with it

when she comes to visit the tomb i'm gonna pretend to be the gardener
and then i'm gonna go BOO! haha it's just me

you're going to reveal the great mystery of conquering the grave with a prank
also she is totally going to beat the shit out of you

      it's a very hilarious goof-'em-up

           like honestly if not now when
        this is basically an unprecedented chance for prankings
             i have some good ones in the chamber i think

i feel like you think that just because you are god crammed into flesh that
you get a pass for being just generally deeply weird as a person

why would she fall for this?

      well she won't, you know, expect it
           i'll do an accent!

she's known you for years she's not face-blind

      oh please she's super rich she won't even look twice at the gardener

you're literally naked and covered with mortal wounds

      maybe i could hold like a shovel

           oh wow actually look how butch i look with this

. . . it's very trade i am not going to lie

      i missed you

    i missed you too

and when the sun has burst fully through the portal
of your tomb i see a frantic mary her sister martha
and your mother crest the garden gate

i am still raw from you and wearing the white of
your shroud and when i speak i still feel your tongue
there

    don't be afraid
    he is risen. he is not here

    we will meet again where we began

and they ran away
terrified

if any take away from these things
        god shall take away their suffering
if any add unto these things
        god shall add unto their joys

            a teacher spoke to me and said
            a holy book that falls apart belongs to someone who will not

            speak again the words our saviour taught us
            take and read and speak again
            speak again
            speak yet again
                    read and speak and take again

                    sing a new song unto the lord

when i dream of what came after, i see a dawn sky, a flash, and then a sound like all the ocean crammed into the fragile spiral of a shell

peter andrew james and i had returned to the place where it began in little dingy dinghy galilee: old wood and gull cry. shrunk to us now, like playing in a childhood bathtub with antique happy meal toys. with us were the sullen twin and sarcastic nathaniel and philip who had served the dunker: a lumpy cluster of unfamiliar calluses and thick beards just beginning to whiten for the harvest, all crammed in mom's kitchen figuring out how to work the electric kettle, then huddled in dad's old boat. peter had wanted to fish again. just to remember. slinking back. history indulging a habit

all night and into day we had caught nothing. but as we hauled the cold wet cabling of our nets by armfuls back into the ship we heard a bark from the faraway shore

> hey guys! nothing yet?
>> try again
>> try again for me

and i knew our master's voice. and the net we cast near tore from its freight. as we paddled back we jumped, plunging diving cannonballing face-planting each by each into the water in a laughing spray, hauling a boat overloaded with fish ashore, our clip-in crowns and zip-tie halos rinsing away in a consecrated confusion of chests and thighs and arms— swimmers in icy january epiphany chasing a golden gilted cross tossed at the churning seashore, squeezing ourselves into each other in the sea-froth milk and spume

and as we crested and sculled in splash and foam and tug my brother began to sing a song of my mother's, and the others heard and joined in uplifted thumping round, the chanty chorus flying flung from the troubled waters to strike the rocks and stones of the cliff and come redounding back upon our heads: a hum, a hosanna in the highest

spattering on shore like wet dogs we found a fire of warm coals sparking sparkling in the dawn on sandy stone and on the stumpy shale altar beach where you had set your throne was warm bread and a dented thermos full of cream and coffee steam and you: in your too-small t-shirt and coarse linen blanket weave-wide and shivering, the frisking lamb of god

      all right hurry the fuck up
      i'm hungry

and there was song and forgivenesses and breakfast in profusion and the
sun came hurtling suddenly over the glass of the sea saying again to the day

                                                              wait
    if this is the last
    if this is the end
    i don't know how to say goodbye to you

    i only know this:
    i will never love anyone anything
    like you the same again

    oh
    no

                never the same
                never again
    each time different
    each wave still the sea
                lathing bottlecaps and feathers
                making all things old and new

    this will all end in white
    till then:

                orbits and counter-orbits
                and widening gyres
                and going forth, to multiply

    split the wood i am beside you
    lift the stone i will be there
    an army of lovers will never be defeated

when you eat
when you love
there i am

                in words
                in beginnings
                good even when it's bad

i am with you always
till the age's end

        it's you and me-handsome

      only love
      as i have loved you

      and you were gone
      like a fist when you open your hand

having loved his own which were in the world
he loved them unto the end

what i heard. what i saw. what i handled and touched
    the sting and seed and shiver

who made me taste of him
                who was like honey in my mouth
                who filled my entrails with his bitterness

all these things i write to you that your joy may be full

god is light and in him is no darkness
            love your brother, sister, mother, friend
            come out of stumbling dark

for i know that we can be forgiven
            that even if our own hearts condemn us
            god is greater than our hearts

        that this world where you have suffered is passing away
                a new heaven and a new earth streak towards us
        and there is nothing lost

        in the beginning was the word
        we are its iteration

        he has on earth
                no eyes now but ours
                no hands now but ours
                no feet now but ours

little children
            love one another

why do you look for the living among the dead?
he is not here. he is risen

    go out and find him

ACKNOWLEDGEMENTS

This book owes its existence to many hands beyond my own, across years and centuries. It is impossible to recognize each of them. However, I will hazard to thank:

My editor, Jordan Ginsberg, without whom this book would likely still be in a drawer. His patience and kindness in coaxing it from the dark first in 2019 for Hazlitt and through the isolated years of the pandemic have been invaluable. Thanks too to the entire team at Penguin Random House Canada for their generosity and enthusiasm, including: Haley Cullingham of Strange Light, our designer Jennifer Griffiths, our copy editor John Sweet, our proofreader Gemma Wain, director of marketing Tonia Addison, and publicist Cameron Waller. I am very grateful to have this book in the hands of such a capable and thoughtful team.

My literary agent, Lauren Abramo, who has been a faithful guide and compassionate ear throughout my projects, and has frequently kept faith whenever I have crumbled. Thank you for your hard work, and for always finding time to listen.

This project was honoured in its early short story form by the National Magazine Awards, and was finalized with the financial support of the Ontario Arts Council. For both of these honours along its development, I am extremely grateful.

Our early readers, whose kind words were of great comfort in the months leading to our launch, including: Kai Cheng Thom, David Demchuk, Daniel Lavery, Lin-Manuel Miranda, Chris Stedman, Kris Trujillo, and Chip Zdarsky. I have been honoured to learned from them both about my own writing and through their own art, and my work and life are richer and wiser for both.

To the subscribers, listeners, and commenters of my podcast The Devil's Party I owe a debt I can never repay. Their willingness to challenge old dogma and creaky glosses, refusal to suffer foolishness even from church fathers and saints, their forbearance with my wilder tangents, and their inexhaustible enthusiasm to share their insights and energy have been an immeasurable source of inspiration and renewal. I wish I could thank you all by name, and am blessed that there are simply too many of you. Thank you so much for making me a better scholar and a better reader.

I acknowledge the tradition in which I was raised and educated at St Francis de Sales Catholic Church & School and St Michael's College School. They were not right; they were not kind; they were not safe. But when I wake sometimes the old hymns are still in my ears, and when I pray it's with the prayers they taught me. Thank you for the parts that were beautiful.

To the communities that fostered and nurtured me: my students and teachers in academia, who taught me rigour and appreciation alike, and let me imagine a life of learning how to love and live with art; the queer community of Toronto (and particularly my fellow employees, patrons, and the literary scene of the Glad Day Bookshop), which showed me how much more life could be and with whom I have known the joy of living, suffering, and caring for one another; the film scene of TIFF, the Revue, and the community that has grown around Dumpster Raccoon Cinema, where I learned how much delight can be found in reassessing the artifacts of our culture; the comic book community, who welcomed me with enthusiasm and open hearts, let me come to their cons and onto their podcasts and into their collections. Thank you all.

I of course owe among the greatest debts to my friends and family, who have been my unflagging support throughout the life of this project and have been refuge from it during its more challenging moments. Thanks especially to my sisters Tracey and Christine Oliveira, their partners Christ Gammage and Josh Kolm, my father Antonio and to my mother Maria, who taught me to read and taught me to sing.

Thank you with all my heart to Alex Koppel, the smartest reader and sweetest man I have ever known. Every morning (or, if I am honest, early-to-mid-afternoon) I get to stumble bleary-eyed downstairs and find an impossible miracle of a man with a 100-watt smile under a pile of cats who shouts "good morning" in a happy baritone. It seems impossible. Thank you and Dax and Jacob for giving a lost stray a home.

This project would never have been completed without the baristas and the espresso machines of Neo Coffee Bar, the Black Canary, and Pilot Coffee Roasters of Toronto, the First Sip Café in Andersonville Chicago, and Variety Coffee at Lexington and 85th.

To the community of saints: living and dead, legendary and lost, in whose number we labour and with whom we love. To the forgiveness of sins, each other's and our own. To the resurrection and celebration of the body. And to a new life everlasting.

Let us love one another.

CREDITS